THE HAUNTED SCHOOL

**Look for more Goosebumps books
by R.L. Stine:
(see back of book for a complete listing)**

Goosebumps®

THE HAUNTED SCHOOL

R.L. STINE

AN
APPLE
PAPERBACK

SCHOLASTIC INC.
New York Toronto London Auckland Sydney

A PARACHUTE PRESS BOOK

ISBN 0-590-56897-3

10   9   8   7   6   5   4   3   2   1

Printed in the U.S.A.

First Scholastic printing, September 1997

THE HAUNTED SCHOOL

1

An invisible hand grabbed me and pulled me off the ladder.

I landed on my back on the gym floor with an "*Oooof!*" My head made a loud *THUD* as it banged the floorboards.

I raised myself slowly, blinking hard, trying to shake off the shock. Then I pulled myself up on my elbows and saw Ben Jackson laughing.

Thalia Halpert-Rodis dropped her lipstick into her bag and came running over to me. "Tommy — are you okay?" she demanded.

"Yeah. Fine," I muttered. "I was just testing the floor. You know. Seeing how hard it is."

"It isn't as hard as your head!" Ben joked. "You're going to have to pay for breaking the gym floor!" He laughed again.

"Ha-ha." Thalia rolled her eyes, then made a disgusted face at him. She turned to me. "Don't encourage him, Tommy. He's about as funny as a dead pigeon."

"I think dead pigeons are funny!" Ben insisted.

Thalia rolled her eyes again. Then she grabbed my hand and tugged me to my feet.

I felt so embarrassed. I wanted to go hide under the bleachers.

Why am I always such a total klutz?

No invisible hand pulled me off the ladder. I just fell. That's what I usually do if I find myself on a ladder. I fall off.

Some people are climbers. I'm a faller.

But I really didn't want to look like a geek in front of Thalia and Ben. After all, I just met them. And I really wanted to impress them.

That's why I signed up for the Dance Decorations Committee. I wanted to meet kids. It's hard to make new friends when you start a new school in sixth grade.

Maybe I'd better start at the beginning.

My name is Tommy Frazer and I'm twelve. Just before school started this fall, my dad got married again. And right after the wedding, we moved to Bell Valley.

We had to move so fast, I barely had a chance to say good-bye to my friends. And before I could catch my breath, here I was — the new kid at Bell Valley Middle School.

I didn't know anyone here. I hardly even knew my new mom!

Can you imagine what it's like to suddenly have a new school, a new house, and a new mom?

2

The first couple of days at Bell Valley Middle School were hard. Kids weren't unfriendly. But they already knew who their friends were.

I'm not shy. But it was really impossible to just go up to someone and say, "Hi. Want to be my friend?"

I was pretty lonely the first week or so. Then last Monday morning, Mrs. Borden, the principal, came into our room. She asked if anyone wanted to volunteer for the Dance Decorations Committee. She needed kids to decorate the gym.

My hand was the first to shoot up. I knew it would be a great way to make new friends.

So here I was after school in the gym two days later. Making new friends by falling on my head like a geek.

"Do you think you should see the nurse?" Thalia asked, studying me.

"No. My eyes always roll around like this," I replied weakly. At least I still had my sense of humor.

"The nurse left, anyway," Ben said, checking his watch. "It's late. We're probably the only ones in the building."

Thalia shook out her blond hair. "Let's get back to work," she suggested.

She opened her bag and pulled out her lipstick. I watched her apply a thick coat of red to her lips, even though they were already red. Then she brushed some kind of orangey powder on her cheeks.

3

Ben shook his head but didn't say anything.

Yesterday, I heard other kids teasing Thalia about her makeup and lipstick. They said she was the only girl in sixth grade who uses that stuff every day.

They were pretty mean to her. One girl said, "Thalia thinks she's painting a masterpiece."

Another girl said, "Thalia couldn't go to gym class because she had to wait for her face to dry."

A boy said, "Her face must be broken. That's why she's always fixing it!"

Everyone laughed really hard.

Thalia didn't seem to mind all the jokes and teasing. I guess she's used to it.

Before school this morning, I heard some kids saying that Thalia was stuck-up. That she thought she was *soooo* beautiful, and that's why she was always paying so much attention to her looks.

She didn't seem stuck-up to me. She seemed really nice. She was pretty awesome looking too. I wondered why she thought she needed to wear makeup at all.

Thalia and Ben look a lot alike. They could be brother and sister, but they're not.

They are both tall and thin. And they both have blue eyes and curly blond hair.

I'm short and a little chubby. And I have black hair that sticks straight out like straw. It's real tough hair. I can brush it for hours, but it still goes wherever it wants.

My new mom says I'll be really handsome as soon as I lose my baby fat. I don't think that was a very good compliment.

Anyway, Thalia, Ben, and I were painting some big banners to go up on the gym wall. Thalia and I were working together on a banner that read BELL VALLEY ROCKS!

Ben started to paint a poster that read DANCE TILL YOU PUKE! But Mrs. Borden poked her head in and asked him to think of a better slogan.

He groaned and grumbled and started over. Now his poster read WELCOME, EVERYONE!

"Hey — where's the red paint?" Thalia called to Ben.

"Huh?" He was down on his hands and knees, using a thick brush to paint the W in WELCOME.

Thalia and I were also down on the floor, painting the black outlines to our poster. She climbed to her feet and stared down at Ben. "Didn't you bring any red paint down to the gym? I only see black."

"I thought you were bringing it," he replied. He pointed to a stack of cans under the basketball hoop. "What are those?"

"All black," she told him. "I asked you to bring down some red — remember? I want to put red in the middle of the letters. Black and red are the school colors, you know."

"Duh," Ben muttered. "Well, I'm not going upstairs for it, Thalia. The art room is on the third floor."

5

"I'll go!" I volunteered, a bit too eagerly.

They both stared at me.

"I mean, I don't mind," I added. "I can use the exercise."

"You really *did* hit your head — didn't you!" Ben joked.

"Do you remember where the art room is?" Thalia asked.

I set down my brush. "Yeah. I think so. You go up the stairs in back — right?"

Thalia nodded. Her curly blond hair bounced whenever she moved her head. "Right. You go up three flights to the top floor. Then you go straight down the hall to the back. Turn right. Then turn right again. And it's at the back."

"No problem," I said. I started jogging to the double gym doors.

"Bring at least two cans!" she called after me. "And some clean brushes."

"And bring me a Coke!" Ben called. He laughed. What a joker.

I started running at full speed to the exit. I'm not sure why I started to run. I guess I was trying to impress Thalia.

I lowered my shoulder. And burst through the double doors.

And barreled at full speed into a girl standing in the hall.

"Hey —!" She let out a startled cry as we both toppled to the floor.

I landed on top of her with a groan.

Her head made a loud *CRACK* as it hit the concrete floor.

Stunned, we both lay there for a second. Then I rolled off her and scrambled to my feet.

"Sorry," I managed to choke out. I reached out to help her up.

But she angrily shoved my hand away and climbed up without my help.

As she stood, I saw that she was at least a foot taller than me. Tall and broad-shouldered and powerful looking, she reminded me of those women wrestlers on TV.

She had white-blond hair, which had fallen over her face. She was dressed all in black. And she stared at me furiously with steel-gray eyes.

Frightening eyes.

"I'm really sorry," I repeated, taking a step back as I stared up at her.

She took a heavy step toward me. Then another. Those cold gray eyes froze me against the wall.

She scowled. And moved closer.

"Wh-what are you going to do?" I stammered.

2

I pressed my back tight against the wall. "What are you going to do?" I repeated.

"I'm going to walk home — if you'll ever *let* me!" she growled. She spun away, her hands squeezed into big fists.

"I *said* I was sorry!" I called after her.

She vanished up the stairs without turning back.

Those weird gray eyes stayed in my mind.

I gave her time to leave the building. Then I started up the stairs.

It was a long climb to the top floor. My legs still felt a little shaky from running into that strange girl. And it was kind of eerie, being the only person up here.

My shoes thudded on the hard steps, and the sound thundered in the empty stairwell. The halls stretched out like long, dark tunnels.

I was out of breath when I finally reached the landing on the third floor. I started down the hall, humming to myself. My voice sounded hollow in the empty hall. It echoed off the long row of gray lockers.

I stopped humming as I made my first right turn. I passed an empty teachers' lounge. A computer lab. Then some rooms that looked empty.

Another right turn took me into a narrow hall with wooden floors that creaked and groaned under my shoes.

I stopped outside the room at the end of the hall. A small hand-lettered sign beside the door read ART ROOM.

I grabbed the doorknob and started to pull open the door.

But I stopped when I heard voices inside the room.

Startled, I gripped the doorknob and listened. I heard a boy and a girl. They were talking softly. I couldn't make out their words. But the kids sounded like Thalia and Ben.

What are they doing up here? I wondered.

Why did they follow me? How did they get up here before I did?

I pushed open the door and stepped inside. "Hey, guys —" I called. "What's going on?"

My mouth dropped open. The room was empty.

"Hey —" I called. "Are you guys in here?"

No reply.

My eyes darted around the big room. Golden afternoon sunlight poured in through the windows.

The long art tables stood clean and empty. Some clay pots were drying on the window ledge. A mobile made of wire hangers and soup cans hung from the ceiling light.

Weird, I thought, shaking my head. I heard voices in here. I know I did.

Are Thalia and Ben playing a little joke on me? I wondered. Are they hiding up here?

I made my way quickly to the big supply closet and pulled open the door. "Caught you!" I cried.

No. No one in there.

I stared into the dark closet. Am I starting to hear voices? I wondered. Maybe my fall off the ladder was worse than I'd thought!

I reached up and pulled the chain to turn on the closet light. On both sides of me, shelves of art supplies reached to the ceiling. I spotted the red paint we needed and started to slide a few cans off the shelf.

But I stopped when I heard a girl laugh.

Then a boy said something. He sounded excited. He was talking rapidly. But I couldn't make out the words.

I spun back to the art room. No one there.

"Hey — where are you?" I called.

Silence now.

I pulled a paint can off the shelf and tucked it under my arm. Then I grabbed another can with my free hand.

"Hey —!" I called out when I heard the voices again.

"This isn't funny!" I cried. "Where are you hiding?"

No reply.

They must be in the next room, I decided. I carried the paint cans out into the art room and set them down on the teacher's desk. Then I crept into the hall.

I stopped at the next door and poked my head into the room. It was some kind of storage room. Boxes marked FRAGILE were stacked against one wall.

No one there.

I checked the room across the hall. No one there, either.

As I walked back to the art room, I heard the voices again.

The girl was shouting now. And then the boy shouted too.

It sounded as if they were calling for help. But for some reason their voices seemed muffled, kind of far away.

My heart started to beat a little faster. My throat suddenly felt dry.

Who is playing this joke on me? I wondered. Everyone has gone home. The whole building is empty. So who is up here? And why can't I find them?

11

"Ben? Thalia?" I shouted. My voice echoed off the long wall of gray lockers. "Are you up here?"

Silence.

I took a deep breath and stepped back into the art room. I'm just going to ignore them, I decided.

I hoisted up the two cans of paint and made my way back out into the hall. I glanced quickly both ways, thinking I might see Thalia and Ben.

A shadow leaned out from an open doorway.

I froze and stared.

"Who — who's there?" I called.

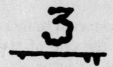

3

A man backed out of the doorway, pulling a large vacuum cleaner. He wore a gray uniform and had the stub of an unlit cigar clenched in his teeth.

The janitor.

I sighed and made my way to the stairs. I don't think he saw me.

The stairway curved halfway down. I started down the steps, but I stopped in front of a large bulletin board on the wall. I glanced over the notices of school events, a calendar, and a lost-and-found list.

Oh, wow. I'm in trouble. I don't remember seeing this on my way up, I told myself.

I gazed back up to the top of the stairs. Did I take the wrong stairway? Will these stairs take me back to the gym?

Only one way to find out, I decided.

Gripping the paint cans tightly, I turned and continued down.

To my surprise, the stairs ended at the second floor.

I gazed down a long hallway, searching for stairs to take me to the gym in the basement. But I saw only closed classroom doors and long rows of metal lockers.

The paint cans started to feel heavy. My shoulders ached. I set the cans on the floor and took a moment to stretch my arms.

Then I picked up the cans and started walking again, my footsteps ringing in the empty hall. I glanced into the rooms I passed.

Whoa!

A skeleton grinned at me from a doorway.

My mouth dropped open. But I quickly got myself together. "Probably some kind of science lab," I murmured.

I thought I saw a small black cat lurking at the end of a row of lockers. I stopped and squinted down at it. Not a cat. Somebody's black wool ski cap.

"Tommy — what is your problem?" I said out loud.

I never realized how creepy a school building can be after everyone has left. Especially a totally unfamiliar school building.

I turned the corner into another long, empty hall. Still no stairs in sight.

Ben and Thalia must wonder what happened to me, I thought. They must think I got lost.

14

Well . . . I *am* lost.

I passed a display case of shiny sports trophies. A red-and-black pennant draped over the case proclaimed GO, BISONS.

That's our team name. The Bell Valley Bisons.

Aren't bisons big and very slow? And aren't they almost extinct?

What a lame team name!

I continued down the hall, thinking hard. Thinking of better team names. The Bell Valley Hippos . . . the Bell Valley Warthogs . . . the Bell Valley Water Buffalos . . .

That last one made me laugh.

But I stopped laughing when I realized I'd reached the end of the hall. A dead end.

"Hey — !" I called out, my eyes searching the closed doors. Shouldn't there be a stairway here? Some kind of exit?

There appeared to be a narrow doorway. But it was boarded up. Old, rotting boards had been nailed over the entire opening.

I never should have volunteered to get the paint, I told myself. This school building is too big, and I don't know my way around.

Thalia and Ben are probably fed up by now.

I gazed down the long hall. Two unmarked doors stood side by side against one wall. They didn't appear to be classroom doors.

I decided to try one.

I leaned forward and pushed a door with my

shoulder. And stumbled into a large, dimly lit room.

"Whoa — where *am* I?" My voice sounded small and shrill. Squinting into the gray light, I saw a crowd of kids staring back at me!

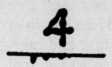

4

The kids stared back at me so stiffly, so still... still as statues.

And then I realized they *were* statues!

Statues of kids. At least two dozen of them.

They were old-fashioned looking. Their clothes were funny, like from an old movie. The boys wore sports jackets and very wide neckties. The girls' jackets all had wide shoulder pads. Their skirts came down to their ankles.

I lowered the paint cans to the floor. Then I took a few cautious steps into the room.

The statues were so real looking, so lifelike. More like department-store mannequins than statues. Their glass eyes glistened. Their red mouths were set sternly, not smiling.

I stepped up to the statue of a boy about my age and grabbed the sleeve of his jacket. Real cloth. Not sculpted stone or plaster.

It was so dark in the room. Hard to see clearly.

I reached into the pocket of my khakis and pulled out my red plastic lighter.

I know, I know. I'm not supposed to have a lighter. There's no reason why I would have one except my grandfather gave me the lighter a few weeks before he died. And I've carried it around with me as a good luck charm ever since.

I flicked the lighter and raised the flame to the boy's face. The skin was so real. It even had tiny pimples on one cheek and a scar under the chin.

I closed the lighter and slipped it back in my pocket. Then I touched the boy's face. Smooth and cool, carved or molded out of some kind of plaster.

I rubbed my finger over one of his eyes. Some kind of glass or plastic.

I tugged at the back of his dark brown hair. It started to slide off.

A wig.

Beside him stood a statue of a tall, thin girl in a black sweater, and a long, straight black skirt down to her ankles. I gazed up into her dark, shiny eyes. She appeared to stare back at me.

So sad. Her expression seemed so sad to me.

Why weren't any of these statues smiling?

I squeezed her hand. Cool plaster.

Why are these statues here? I wondered. Who put them here in this hidden room? Is it some sort of art project?

I stepped back — and spotted an engraved sign

over the door. My eyes moved quickly over the big, block letters:

CLASS OF 1947

I stared at the sign. Read it again.

Then I turned back to the roomful of statues.

And one of the statues called out: "What are *you* doing here?"

5

"Huh?" I let out a loud gasp.

"What are you *doing* in here, young man?" the voice repeated.

Blinking hard, I whirled around.

And saw Mrs. Borden, the principal, standing in the open doorway.

"You — you're not a statue!" I blurted out.

She moved quickly into the room, holding a clipboard against the front of her sweater. "No, I'm not," she replied without smiling.

She glanced down at the two paint cans on the floor. Then she stepped up beside me, her eyes studying me.

Mrs. Borden is very short. She is only an inch or two taller than me. And she's kind of chubby. She has curly black hair and a round, pink face. She always seems to be blushing.

Some kids told me that she's really nice. I met her only for a moment when I showed up at Bell Valley my first morning.

That morning, she was all upset about a pack of dogs that were swarming over the playground and frightening the little kids. She didn't have time to talk to me.

Now she stood so close to me, I could smell the peppermint on her breath. "Tommy, I think you must be lost," she said softly.

I nodded. "Yeah. I guess," I murmured.

"Where are you supposed to be?" she asked, still clutching the clipboard to her chest.

"The gym," I replied.

She finally smiled. "You're a long way from the gym. This is the entrance to the old building. The gym is in the new building, way on the other side." She gestured with the clipboard.

"I took the wrong stairs," I explained. "I was coming from the art room, and —"

"Oh, right. You're on the Dance Decorations Committee," she interrupted. "Well, let me show you how to get back downstairs."

I turned to the statues. They all stood so still, so silently. They seemed to be eavesdropping on Mrs. Borden and me.

"What *is* this room?" I asked.

She put a hand on my shoulder and started to move me toward the door. "It's a private room," she said softly.

"But what *is* it?" I repeated. "I mean — these statues. Who are these kids? Are they real kids or something?"

21

She didn't reply. Her hand tightened on my shoulder as she guided me to the door.

I stopped to pick up the paint cans. When I glanced back at Mrs. Borden, her expression had changed.

"This is a very sad room, Tommy," she said, her voice just above a whisper. "These kids were the very first class in the school."

"The class of nineteen forty-seven?" I asked, glancing at the sign.

The principal nodded. "Yes. Just about fifty years ago. There were twenty-five kids in the school. And one day . . . one day, they all disappeared."

"Huh?" Startled by her words, I dropped the paint cans to the floor.

"They vanished, Tommy," Mrs. Borden continued, turning her gaze to the statues. "Vanished into thin air. One minute they were here in school. The next minute, they were gone . . . forever. Never seen again."

"But — but —" I sputtered. I didn't know what to say. How could twenty-five kids vanish?

Mrs. Borden sighed. "It was a terrible tragedy," she said softly. "A terrible mystery. The parents . . . the poor parents . . ."

Her voice caught in her throat. She took a deep breath. "They were so heartbroken. The parents had the school boarded up. Closed forever. The town built a new school around it. The old building has stood empty ever since that horrible day."

"And these statues?" I asked.

"A local artist made them," Mrs. Borden replied. "He used a class photo. A photo of everyone. The artist used the photo to make these statues. A tribute to the missing children."

I stared at the roomful of statues. Kids. Vanished kids.

"Weird," I muttered.

I picked up the paint cans. Mrs. Borden opened the door.

"I — I didn't mean to come in here," I apologized. "I didn't know . . ."

"No problem," she replied. "This building is very big and very confusing."

I led the way out to the hall. She closed the door carefully behind us. "Follow me," she said. The heels of her shoes clicked loudly on the hard floor as she walked, swinging the clipboard at her side.

She walked really fast for a tiny person. Holding a paint can in each hand, I had to struggle to keep up with her.

"How are you getting along, Tommy?" she asked. "Aside from getting lost, I mean."

"Fine," I said. "Everyone's been really great."

We turned a corner. I had to jog to catch up to her. We turned another corner. Into a brighter hallway. The tile walls were a bright yellow. The linoleum floor gleamed.

"This is where you meant to go," Mrs. Borden announced. "And there is the stairway down to the gym." She pointed the way, then smiled at me.

I thanked her and hurried off.

I couldn't wait to get back to the gym. I hoped Thalia and Ben weren't angry about how long it took me. I was really eager to ask them about the class of 1947. I wanted to hear what they knew about all those missing kids.

Holding the cans of red paint, I made my way down the two flights of stairs to the basement. It all looked familiar now.

I ran past the lunchroom to the double gym doors at the end of the hall. Pushed open the doors with my shoulder. And burst into the gym.

"Hey — I'm back!" I called. "I —"

The words caught in my throat. Thalia and Ben were sprawled facedown on the gym floor.

6

"Oh, nooooooo!" I let out a wail of horror.

The paint cans fell from my hands and clattered heavily to the gym floor.

One of the cans rolled in my path, and I stumbled over it as I hurtled toward my new friends. "Thalia! Ben!" I screamed.

They both giggled.

And raised their heads from the floor, grinning.

Ben opened his mouth in a long, phony yawn.

"We got so tired waiting for you, we fell asleep!" Thalia declared.

They both laughed again. Ben shot Thalia a high five.

They both climbed to their feet. Thalia hurried over to her purse. She pulled out a lipstick tube and began applying another red coat to her lips.

Grinning, Ben narrowed his eyes at me. "You got lost — right?"

I nodded unhappily. "Yeah. So? Big deal," I muttered.

"I win the bet!" Ben cried happily. He held out a hand to Thalia. "Pay up."

"Whoa! I don't believe you two!" I exclaimed. "You bet on whether I got lost or not?"

"We were pretty bored," Thalia confessed. She handed Ben a dollar.

He shoved it into his jeans pocket. Then he glanced up at the big scoreboard clock. "Oh, wow!" he cried. "I'm late! I promised my brother I'd get home by five."

He ran to the bleachers and started gathering up his backpack and jacket.

"Hey, wait —" I called. "I want to tell you what I saw upstairs! I mean, it was so weird. I —"

"Later," he said, pulling on his jacket as he jogged toward the double doors.

"But what about the red paint?" I cried.

"I'll drink it tomorrow!" he shouted. Then he disappeared out the doors.

I watched them bang shut. Then I turned to Thalia.

"He's pretty funny sometimes," she said. "I mean, sometimes he makes me laugh."

"Ha-ha," I muttered.

I picked up the cans of red paint and carried them over to our banners on the floor. "Sorry it took me so long," I told her. "But —"

She was brushing some kind of makeup onto her eyelids. "You saw something weird upstairs?" she asked, glancing at me over the little round mirror she held in her free hand.

"Well, first I ran into the hall and knocked over this weird girl," I told her.

Thalia narrowed her eyes at me. "What weird girl?"

"I don't know her name," I replied. "She's big — a lot taller than me. And really tough looking. And she has the weirdest gray eyes, and —"

"Greta?" Thalia asked. "You knocked over Greta?"

"Is that her name?" I replied.

"Dressed in black?" Thalia asked. "Greta always dresses in black."

"Yeah. That was her," I said. "I knocked her flat. Then I fell on top of her. Smooth move, huh?"

"Watch out for her, Tommy," Thalia warned. "Greta is definitely weird." She started to roll up her banner. "So what happened to you upstairs?"

"I heard something," I told her. "When I got to the art room. I heard voices. Kids' voices. But when I went inside the room, there was no one there."

"Huh?" Thalia's mouth dropped open. "You — you *heard* them?" she stammered.

I nodded.

"You really heard them?"

"Yes. Who were they?" I demanded. "I kept searching for them. All over the third floor. I heard them, but I couldn't see them. And then Mrs. Borden —"

I stopped talking when I saw that Thalia had tears in her eyes.

"Hey — what's wrong?" I asked.

She didn't answer me. She spun away — and ran from the gym.

7

A few days later, Thalia had a run-in with Greta. And it almost turned violent.

It was Thursday afternoon. Mr. Devine, our teacher, received a message from the office. He read the message a few times, moving his lips as he read. Then, muttering to himself, he left the room.

It was near the end of the school day. I guess everyone was tired of sitting in school. We were all ready to break out of there.

So as soon as Mr. Devine disappeared, everyone kind of exploded. I mean, guys jumped up and started running around the room. Doing funny dance moves and just goofing.

One kid turned on a boom box he had hidden under his desk and cranked the music up. Some girls were laughing wildly about something in the back of the room, tossing their heads and slapping their hands on their desks.

I sit in the back row since I'm a new kid. Ben

was absent. I think he had a dentist appointment or something.

So since I didn't really know anyone else yet, I sort of was left out of all the fun.

I tapped my hand to the music and pretended I was having a good time. But actually, I felt kind of awkward and lonely. And I secretly wished that Mr. Devine would come back so that things could return to normal.

I stared out the window for a while. It was a cloudy autumn day. Very windy. The swirling wind gusts sent red and yellow leaves sailing and twisting over the playground.

I stared at them for a while. Then I turned back into the room, and my eyes landed on Thalia in the front row.

She wasn't paying any attention to all the dancing and joking and wild laughter. She had her little mirror raised to her face and was slicking a layer of lipstick onto her lips.

I waved and tried to get her attention. I wanted to know if she and I were going to work on decorations after school in the gym.

I tried calling to her. But she couldn't hear me over all the noise. She stared into her little mirror and didn't turn around.

I started to stand up and walk over to her — when I saw Greta lean over Thalia's desk and grab the lipstick tube from her hand. Greta laughed and said something to Thalia. She held the lipstick tube out of Thalia's reach.

Thalia let out an angry scream. She swiped at the lipstick. But she wasn't fast enough to grab it back.

Greta's gray eyes glinted with excitement. She laughed and heaved it to a guy across the room.

"Give that back!" Thalia shrieked.

She leaped to her feet. Her eyes were wild, and her face was pale.

"Give that back! Give it! Give it!"

With a furious growl, Thalia dove across the row of desks and tried to tackle the boy.

Laughing, he dodged away from her and tossed the tube back to Greta.

The metal tube hit a desk and bounced onto the floor.

Thalia hurtled herself to the floor, grabbing at it wildly with both hands.

I was halfway to the front of the room. As she and Greta wrestled on the floor for the lipstick, I gaped at Thalia in shock.

What is the big deal? I wondered. Why is she so desperate to get that tube back? It's only lipstick, after all.

Other kids were watching the struggle. I saw the girls at the back of the room laughing at Thalia. They were the ones who had teased her about wearing makeup.

Some kids cheered as Greta came up with the lipstick. She raised it in her big fist.

Thalia screamed and grabbed at it.

And then Greta raised the lipstick tube higher toward Thalia's face.

And drew a red smiley face on Thalia's forehead.

Thalia had tears in her eyes now. I saw that she was totally losing it.

I didn't really understand why she was so *insane* about it. But I decided I had to do something.

Hero time for Tommy Frazer.

"Hey — give that back to her!" I boomed.

I took a deep breath and stepped forward to teach Greta a lesson.

Greta was holding the lipstick tube high over her head, pushing Thalia away with her other hand.

"Give it back to her!" I insisted, trying to sound tough. "It isn't funny, Greta. Give Thalia the lipstick."

I jumped up — and grabbed the hand with the lipstick in it.

I heard some kids cheering and clapping. I didn't know which of us they were cheering.

Using both hands, I started to pry the tube from Greta's big hand.

And that's when Mr. Devine returned to the room.

"What's going on?" he demanded.

I turned to see him glaring at me through his round, black-frame eyeglasses.

I lowered my hands from Greta's fist. The lipstick tube dropped to the floor. It rolled under Thalia's desk.

With a tiny cry, she dove for it.

"What's happening in here?" Mr. Devine moved quickly to the front of the room.

"Tommy, why are you up here?" the teacher demanded. Behind his thick glasses, his eyes looked as big as tennis balls! "Why did you leave your seat?"

"I was just...uh...getting something," I choked out.

"He was helping me," Thalia chimed in. I gazed down at her. She seemed a lot calmer now that she had her lipstick back.

Meanwhile, my heart was pounding like crazy.

"Get back to your seats, everyone," Mr. Devine ordered. "I should be able to leave the room for two minutes without everyone going berserk." He turned his stare on Greta.

"Just goofing around," she muttered. She tossed back her white-blond hair and dropped heavily into her seat.

I slumped back to my desk and took deep breaths. I wanted to ask Thalia what the big deal was about her lipstick. But she didn't turn around.

It took a few more seconds for Mr. Devine to get everyone calmed down. Then he glanced up at the clock above the chalkboard.

"We have twenty more minutes until the bell rings," he announced. "I have to take care of some paperwork at my desk. So I'd like you to use the time for quiet reading."

He pulled off his glasses and blew a speck off

34

one of the lenses. His eyes looked like tiny marbles when he took the glasses off.

"Your book reports are all due on Monday," he reminded us. "So this would be a good time to do some reading."

There was a lot of chair scraping and book bag thudding and thumping as we all pulled out our reading books. A few seconds later, the room fell silent.

I was reading a book of short stories by Ray Bradbury for my book report. I'm not a science-fiction freak or anything. But these stories were really good. Most of them had surprise endings, which I really like.

I tried to concentrate on the story I was reading. It was about these kids who live on a planet where it never stops raining. A very sad story. They never ever see the sun shine. And they can never go outside to play.

I read a couple of pages. And then I nearly dropped the book when I heard a voice. A girl's voice. Very soft — but very near.

"*Please help me,*" she cried. "*Help me. . . .*"

Startled, I slammed the book shut and glanced around.

Who said that?

My eyes landed on Thalia. Was she calling to me?

No. She had her face buried in a book.

"*Help me — please!*" I heard the girl plead again.

I spun around. No one there.

"Did anyone hear that?" I asked, more loudly than I'd planned.

Mr. Devine raised his eyes from his papers. "Tommy? What did you say?"

"Did anyone hear that girl?" I asked. "Calling for help?"

A few kids laughed. Thalia turned and frowned at me.

"I didn't hear anything," Mr. Devine replied.

"No. Really," I insisted. "I heard her. She said, 'Please help me.'"

Mr. Devine *tsk-tsked*. "You're too young to start hearing voices."

Some more kids laughed. I didn't think it was very funny.

I sighed and picked up my book. I couldn't wait for the bell to ring. I really wanted to get out of that classroom.

I thumbed through the book, trying to find my page.

But before I found it, I heard the girl's voice again.

So soft and near. And so unhappy.

"Help me. Please. Please, somebody — help me."

9

On the night of the school dance, Ben, Thalia, and I got to the gym early. With only an hour to go, we were busily putting the finishing touches on the decorations.

I thought it all looked pretty great.

We had banners strung out in the hall outside the gym. And two big banners in the gym, proclaiming BELL VALLEY ROCKS! and WELCOME, EVERYONE!

We tied huge bouquets of helium balloons to the two basketball hoops. The balloons were all red and black, of course. And we had red and black crepe-paper streamers on the walls and over the bleachers.

Thalia and I had spent days painting a big poster of a bison giving the thumbs-up sign. Underneath the bison, it said BISONS RULE! in red and black letters.

Thalia and I aren't very good artists. The bison didn't really look much like the photos of bisons we'd found in books. Ben said it looked more like a cow that had been sick for a long time. But we hung the poster up, anyway.

Now, the three of us were arranging a red-and-black crepe-paper tablecloth over the refreshment table. I glanced up at the scoreboard clock. Seven thirty. The dance was scheduled to start at eight.

"We still have a lot to do," I said.

Ben tugged his end of the paper tablecloth too hard. I heard a soft ripping sound.

"Ooops," he said. "Anybody bring any tape?"

"It's no problem," Thalia told him. "We'll just cover the torn part with soda bottles or something."

I glanced at the clock again. "When is the band supposed to arrive?"

"Any minute," Thalia replied. "They were supposed to get here early to set up."

Some kids had formed a band called Grunt. It was sort of a strange band — five guitar players and a drummer. And I heard some kids saying that three of the guitar players didn't really know how to play.

But Mrs. Borden asked them to perform a few songs at the dance.

It took us a while to get the tablecloth straight. It wasn't quite big enough for the table.

"What's next?" Ben asked. "Do we have decorations for the gym doors?"

Before I could answer, the double doors swung open, and Mrs. Borden came charging in. At first, I didn't recognize her. She wore a shiny bright red party dress. And she had her black curly hair piled up high on her head behind a silver tiara.

Even with her hair piled up, she still wasn't much taller than we were!

Her eyes darted around the gym as she hurried over to us. "It looks great! Just *fabulous*, guys!" she gushed. "Oh, you worked so hard! You did a wonderful job!"

We thanked her.

She slapped a Polaroid camera into my hands. "Take pictures, Tommy," she instructed me. "Snapshots of the decorations. Hurry. Take a whole bunch before people start arriving."

I examined the camera. "Well . . . okay," I agreed. "But Thalia, Ben, and I still have some stuff to do. We have posters for the doors. And we need more balloons over there. And — and —"

Mrs. Borden laughed. "You're a little *stressed!*"

Thalia and Ben laughed too. I could feel my face turning hot. I knew I was blushing.

"Take it easy, Tommy," Mrs. Borden said, patting my shoulder soothingly. "Or you won't survive until the dance."

I forced a smile. "I'm okay," I told her.

Little did I realize that — after all my hard work — I would never see the dance.

10

"Yo! Look out!"

"Move that amp! Hey, Greta — move that amp!"

"Move it yourself!"

"Where's my wa-wa? Did anyone see my wa-wa pedal?"

"I ate it for breakfast!"

"You're not funny. Move that amp!"

The band members arrived while I was snapping Polaroids. And they instantly took over, making a big racket as they set up by the bleachers.

The guitarists were all guys. Greta was the drummer. Seeing her lug her drums across the gym reminded me of the lipstick battle in class on Thursday.

After school, I'd asked Thalia what the big deal was. "Why did you go nuts?" I asked.

"I didn't go nuts!" Thalia insisted. "Greta did. She thinks because she's so big and strong she can just grab whatever she wants."

"She's really weird," I agreed. "But you were so upset —"

"I *like* that lipstick. That's all," Thalia replied. "It's my best lipstick. Why should I let her grab it from me?"

Now Greta, dressed in black as always, was setting up with the rest of the band. They were all laughing and shoving each other around, tossing cables back and forth, tripping over their guitar cases. Acting like big shots because they had a band.

A few other kids started to arrive. I recognized the two girls who were the ticket takers. And a couple of kids from the refreshment committee, who started complaining that somebody ordered only Mountain Dew and no Coke.

I scrambled around, snapping photos of the banners and the balloons. I was setting up to shoot our bison poster — when a loud shout made me spin around.

I saw Greta and one of the guitar players pretending to have a duel with guitars. The other band members were laughing and cheering them on.

Greta had picked up one of the guitars. She and the other guy raised their guitars high over their heads and came charging at each other.

"No — *stop*!" I screamed.

Too late.

Greta's guitar ripped right through the BELL VALLEY ROCKS! banner. Tore it in two!

I let out a loud groan as the two halves of the banner drooped to the floor. I turned and saw the unhappy faces of Thalia and Ben.

"Hey — sorry about that!" Greta called. Then she burst out laughing.

I hurried over to the wrecked banner and picked up one end. Thalia and Ben were right behind me.

"What are we going to do?" I cried. "It's ruined."

"We can't just leave it here hanging over the floor," Thalia said, shaking her head.

"We need it!" I declared.

"Yeah. It's our best banner," Thalia agreed.

"Maybe we can tape it back together," I suggested.

"No problem. We'll tape it together," Ben said. "Come on, Tommy." He grabbed my arm and started to pull me.

I almost dropped Mrs. Borden's Polaroid. "Where are we going?" I demanded.

"Up to the art room, of course," Ben replied. He started jogging to the double gym doors, and I followed.

It won't take long to tape it together, I thought. Then I'll get a ladder from the janitor's closet, and we'll hang it back up.

We stepped out into the hall — and I stopped. Kids were arriving for the dance, hurrying to the gym.

42

"We don't have time to fix the banner!" I told Ben.

"We'll hurry," he said. "No problem."

"But — but the art room is way up on the third floor!" I sputtered. "By the time we get all the way back down to the gym . . ."

"Relax," Ben said. "It won't take that long — if you'd stop complaining. Come on. Let's go!"

Ben was right. I started running down the hall. Kids were pouring into the gym. I knew we had to hurry.

"Hey — not that way!" I heard him calling. "You're going the wrong way, Tommy!"

"I know where I'm going!" I called back. "I went this way last time!"

I ran to the end of the hall and turned a corner.

"Tommy — stop!" Ben called.

"It's up this way!" I called back to him. "This way is faster. I know it."

But I was wrong. I should have listened to Ben. A few seconds later, the hall ended at a boarded-up wall.

"See?" Ben cried breathlessly. "What is your problem? The stairs are back there."

"Okay. I made a mistake," I told him. "I wanted to hurry, that's all."

"But you don't know where you're going!" he said angrily. "Remember, Tommy? You need a road map to find your toes!"

"Very funny," I muttered. I gazed around. "Where are we?"

"I don't know! I can't believe I followed you!" Ben was annoyed. He banged both fists against the boarded-up wall.

"Hey —!"

We both cried out as the rotted, old boards broke away. Startled, Ben stumbled forward — and crashed right through the boards.

They splintered and fell to the floor. And he fell on top of them.

"Oh, wow." I bent to help him up. "Check this out!" I said, peering down a dark hall. "This must be the old school building. The building they closed off."

"Thrills and chills," Ben muttered. He groaned and rubbed his knee. "I scraped my knee on those boards. I think it's bleeding."

I took a few steps into the dark hall. "This school has been closed off for fifty years," I told him. "We're probably the first kids in here since then!"

"Remind me to write that in my diary," Ben growled, still rubbing his knee. "Are we going to the art room or what?"

I didn't answer him. Something on the wall across from us caught my eye. I walked over to it.

"Hey, Ben. Look. An elevator."

"Huh?" He hobbled across the hall to me.

"Do you believe it?" I asked. "They had an elevator in the old school."

"Those kids were lucky," Ben replied.

I pressed the button on the wall. To my surprise, the doors slid open. "Whoa — !" I peered inside. A dusty ceiling lamp clicked on, sending pale white light down through the metal car.

"It's on!" Ben cried. "It's working!"

"Let's take it to the third floor," I urged. "Come on. Why should we walk up all those stairs?"

"But — but —" Ben held back. But I grabbed his shoulders and pushed him inside the elevator. And followed him in.

"This is great!" I exclaimed. "I told you I knew how to get there."

Ben's eyes darted nervously around the narrow gray elevator car. "We shouldn't be doing this," he murmured.

"What could happen?" I replied.

The doors closed silently.

11

"Are we moving?" Ben asked. His eyes rose to the elevator ceiling.

"Of course not," I replied. "We haven't pushed the button yet."

I reached out and pushed the button with a big black 3 on it. "What is your problem, anyway?" I demanded. "Why are you so nervous? We're not robbing a bank or anything. We're just riding an elevator because we're in a hurry."

"The elevator is fifty years old," Ben replied.

"So?" I demanded.

"So . . . we're not moving," Ben said softly.

I pushed the button again. And listened for the hum that meant we were going up.

Silence.

"Let's get out of here," Ben said. "It's not working. I told you we shouldn't try it."

I pushed the button again. Nothing.

I pushed the button marked 2.

"We're wasting time," Ben said. "If we ran up

the stairs, we'd be up there already. The dance is starting, and the stupid banner is trailing on the floor."

I pushed the 3 button again. And the 2 button.

Nothing. No noise. We didn't move.

I pushed the button marked B.

"We don't want to go to the basement!" Ben cried. I heard a little panic start to creep into his voice. "Tommy, why did you push B?"

"Just trying to get it to move," I said. My throat suddenly felt a little dry. I had a knot in the pit of my stomach.

Why weren't we moving?

I pushed all the buttons again. Then I pounded them with my fist.

Ben pulled my hand away. "Nice try, ace," he said sarcastically. "Let's just get out of here, okay? I don't want to miss the whole dance."

"Thalia is probably a little steamed by now," I said, shaking my head. I pushed 3 a few more times.

But we didn't move.

"Just open the doors," Ben insisted.

"Okay. Fine," I agreed unhappily. My eyes swept over the control panel.

"What's wrong?" Ben asked impatiently.

"I — I can't find the DOOR OPEN button," I stammered.

He shoved me out of the way. "Here," he said, gazing over the silvery buttons. "Uh . . ."

47

We both studied the control panel.

"There's *got* to be a DOOR OPEN button," Ben muttered.

"Maybe it's this one with the arrows," I said. I lowered my hand to a button at the bottom of the metal panel. It had two arrows on it that pointed like this: <> .

"Yes. Push it," Ben said. He didn't wait for me to do it. He reached past me and pushed the button hard with his open hand.

I stared at the door, waiting for it to slide open. It didn't move.

I slapped the <> button again. And again.

Nothing.

"How are we going to get *out* of here?" Ben cried.

"Don't panic," I told him. "We'll get the doors open."

"Why shouldn't I panic?" he demanded shrilly.

"Because I want to be the one to panic first!" I declared. I thought my little joke would make him laugh and calm him down. After all, *he* was always making jokes.

But he didn't even smile. And he didn't take his eyes off the dark elevator doors.

I pushed the <> button one more time. I kept it pressed in with my thumb. The doors didn't open.

I pushed the 3 and the 2 buttons. I pushed the 1 button.

Nothing. Silence. The buttons didn't even click.

Ben's eyes bulged. He cupped his hands around his mouth. "Help us!" he screamed. "Can anybody hear me? Help us!"

Silence.

Then I spotted the red button at the top of the control panel. "Ben — look," I said. I pointed to the red button.

"An emergency button!" he exclaimed happily. "Go ahead, Tommy. Push it! It's probably an alarm. Someone will hear it and come rescue us!"

I pushed the red button.

I didn't hear an alarm.

But the elevator started to hum.

I heard the clank of gears. The floor vibrated beneath our feet.

"Hey — we're moving!" Ben cried happily.

I let out a cheer. Then I raised my hand to slap him a high five.

But the elevator jerked hard, and I fell against the wall.

"Uh-oh," I murmured, pulling myself up straight. I turned to Ben. We stared at each other in wide-eyed silence, not believing what was happening.

The elevator wasn't moving up. Or down. It was moving *sideways*.

12

The elevator rumbled and shook. I grabbed the wooden railing on the side. Gears clanked noisily. The floor vibrated beneath my shoes.

We stared at each other, realizing what was happening. Neither of us spoke.

Ben finally broke the silence. "This is impossible," he murmured. His words came out in a choked whisper.

"Where is it taking us?" I asked softly, gripping the rail so hard that my hands hurt.

"It's impossible!" Ben repeated. "It can't be happening. Elevators only go up and —"

The car jolted hard as we came to a very sudden stop.

"Whoooa!" I let out a cry as my shoulder slammed into the elevator wall.

"Next time, we're taking the stairs," Ben growled.

The doors slid open.

We peered out. Into total blackness.

"Are we in the basement?" Ben asked, sticking his head out the door.

"We didn't go down," I replied. A shiver ran down the back of my neck. "We didn't go up or down. So . . ."

"We're still on the first floor." Ben finished my sentence for me. "But why is it so dark here? I can't believe this is happening!"

We stepped out of the elevator.

I waited for my eyes to adjust to the darkness. But they couldn't adjust. It was too dark.

"There must be a light switch," I said. I ran my hand along the wall. I could feel the outline of tiles. But no light switch.

I swept both hands up and down the wall. No. No light switch.

"Let's get out of here," Ben urged. "We don't want to get trapped here. We can't see a thing."

I was still searching for the light. "Okay," I agreed. I lowered my hand and started back to the elevator.

I heard the doors slide shut.

"No!" I let out a sharp cry.

Ben and I banged on the elevator doors. Then I felt along the wall for the button to open the doors.

Panicked, my hand trembled. I swept my open palm all along the wall on both sides of the closed doors.

No button. No elevator button.

I turned and leaned my back against the wall. I

was suddenly breathing hard. My heart pounded.

"I can't believe this is happening," Ben muttered.

"Would you *please* stop saying that!" I demanded. "It *is* happening. We're here. We don't know where. But we're here."

"But if we can't call the elevator, how do we get out of here?" Ben whined.

"We'll find our way," I told him. I took a deep breath and held it. I decided I had to be the calm one since he was being so whiny and scared.

I listened hard. "I can't hear any music or voices or anything. We must be far away from the gym."

"Well . . . what do we do?" Ben cried. "We can't just stand here!"

My mind whirred. I squinted into the darkness, hoping to make out the shape of a door or a window. *Anything!*

But the blackness that surrounded us was darker than the sky on a starless night.

I pressed my back against the cool tile wall. "I know," I said. "We'll keep against the wall."

"And?" Ben whispered. "And we'll do *what*?"

"We'll move along the wall," I continued. "We'll move along the wall until we come to a door. A door to a room with a light. Then maybe we'll be able to figure out where we are."

"Maybe," Ben replied. He didn't sound hopeful.

"Stick close behind me," I instructed him.

He bumped up against me.

"Not *that* close!" I said.

"I couldn't help it. I can't see!" he cried.

Moving slowly — very slowly — we started walking. I kept my right hand on the wall, sliding it along the tiles as we walked.

We'd only taken a few steps when I heard a sound behind me. A cough.

I stopped and turned around. "Ben — was that you?"

"Huh?" He bumped into me again.

"Did you cough?" I asked softly.

"No," he replied.

I heard another cough. Then a loud whisper.

"Uh . . . Ben . . ." I said, grabbing his shoulder. "Guess what? We're not alone."

13

We both gasped as the lights came on. Dim and gray at first.

I blinked several times and waited for the light to brighten.

But it didn't.

I stared out. We were in a room! A gray classroom. My eyes moved from the black chalkboard to the charcoal-colored teacher's desk. To the dark gray student desks. The pale gray tile walls. Then down to the black-and-gray patterns on the classroom floor.

"Weird," Ben muttered. "My eyes —"

"It's not your eyes," I assured him. "The light is so dim in this room, it makes everything look gray and black."

"It's like being in an old black-and-white movie," Ben declared.

Squinting into the dim light, we started edging toward the classroom door. "Let's get out of here," I suggested. "Before the lights go out again."

We were halfway across the room when I heard another cough. And then a girl's voice rang out. "Hey —!"

Ben and I both stopped. We turned as a girl about our age stepped out from behind a book cabinet.

She stared at us.

We stared back at her.

She was kind of cute, with short, straight black hair and bangs across her forehead. She wore an old-fashioned-looking V-necked sweater, a long, pleated skirt, and black-and-white saddle shoes.

I opened my mouth to say hi. But no sound came out as I noticed her skin. Her skin was as gray as her sweater. And her eyes were gray. And her lips were gray.

She was like the room. She was in black-and-white too!

Ben and I exchanged confused glances. Then I turned back to the girl. She clung to the side of the cabinet, eyeing Ben and me suspiciously.

"Were you hiding back there?" I blurted out.

She nodded. "We heard you coming. But we didn't know who you were."

"*We?*" I asked.

Before she could answer, four more kids — two boys and two girls — jumped out from behind the tall cabinet.

All gray! All in shades of gray!

"Look at them!" one of the boys cried. His eyes bulged as he stared at us.

"I don't believe it!" another boy shouted.

Before Ben and I could move, they rushed forward.

All shouting and crying out at once, they stampeded across the room.

Surrounded us.

Grabbed us.

Pulled at our clothes.

Pulled us. Screaming. Laughing. Shrieking.

Pulled out my shirt. Ripped my sleeve.

"Ben —!" I screamed. "They — they're going to *tear us apart!*"

14

"Look! Look at this!" a girl cried. She held up my shirtsleeve.

Two boys tugged at the rest of my shirt.

I dropped to the floor. Tried to squirm away.

But they had us surrounded.

A girl pulled off one of my shoes.

Ben swung his fist hard, trying to fight them away. His hand smacked the blackboard, and he cried out in pain.

"Stop!" I heard a boy shout over the cries of the others. "Stop it! Get away from them!"

I kicked out with both feet. I saw Ben swing his fist again.

"Stop it!" the boy screamed. "Get away! Come on — stop!"

The kids backed away. The girl dropped my shoe. I grabbed it off the floor.

They took several steps back, moving in a line, staring at us.

"The color!" a girl exclaimed. "So much color!"

"It hurts my eyes!" a boy cried.

"But it's so *beautiful*!" a girl gushed. "It — it's like a dream!"

"Do you still dream in color?" a boy asked her. "My dreams are all in black and white."

Tugging on my shoe, I climbed shakily to my feet. I struggled to straighten my khakis and tuck in my torn shirt.

Ben rubbed the hand he had smacked. His blond hair was matted with sweat. His face was bright red.

"Tommy," he whispered. "What's going on? This is *crazy*!"

I stared at the five kids lined up in front of us.

"No color . . . ," I murmured.

All of them were in black and white. Their clothes, their skin, their eyes, their hair — no color at all. Only shades of gray and black.

As I struggled to catch my breath, I studied them. And realized they didn't look like modern kids, like kids from our school.

The girls all wore skirts, long skirts down to their ankles. The boys wore big-collared sports shirts, tucked into baggy, pleated pants.

Like in an old movie . . . I thought.

And all black and gray.

We all stared at one another for a long while. Then the boy who seemed to be their leader spoke up. "We're all sorry," he said. "You see, we —"

"We didn't mean to hurt you," the girl beside

him interrupted. "It's just that . . . we haven't seen color for so long."

"I just wanted to *touch* it," the girl with black bangs across her forehead added, shaking her head sadly. "I wanted to touch color. It's been so long. So long . . ."

"Did you come to help us?" the first boy asked softly. His gray eyes locked on mine. Pleading eyes.

"Help you?" I replied. "No. No, we didn't. You see —"

"That's too bad," the girl with black bangs said, frowning.

"Huh? Too bad?" I didn't understand. "Why?" I asked.

"Because," replied the girl, "now you can never leave."

15

"Hey — we've already scared them. They think we're a bunch of crazed savages. Don't try to scare them even more, Mary!" the boy scolded.

"I'm not!" she insisted, crossing her arms over the front of her gray sweater. "I just think they should know the truth. I think —"

"The truth?" I interrupted. "What's going on here? This is a joke — right?"

"Yeah. Go ahead. Wipe off the gray powder from your face and tell us it's a joke," Ben chimed in.

The girl named Mary bit her bottom lip. I saw a tear form in her left eye. It brimmed over and ran down her gray cheek. "It's no joke," she choked out.

"Give us a break!" Ben groaned. "Just make the lights brighter, and —"

"That won't help!" the boy cried angrily.

Mary turned to him. She wiped the tear from

her cheek. "I really thought they came to help us," she said in a quivering voice. "I really thought that finally . . . " Her voice trailed off.

Another girl put her arm around Mary.

I shut my eyes for a moment. Squinting into the gray was giving me a headache.

"Will someone tell us what is going on?" I heard Ben demand.

I opened my eyes to see all five gray kids moving across the room toward us.

The leader was a little taller than me. He had wavy black hair, and big black eyes that crinkled at the sides. I saw a small gray scar above one eyebrow. He had broad shoulders beneath his gray T-shirt. He was very athletic looking.

The girl beside him was tall and very thin. She had long gray hair that fell straight down her back. She had sad gray eyes.

"I'm Seth," the boy said. "This is Mary and this is Eloise." He pointed. "Eddie and Mona."

Ben and I introduced ourselves.

"We didn't mean to frighten you," Mary repeated. "But can we touch your colors? We haven't seen color for so long. We just —" Her voice cracked. She turned away.

"Uh . . . Ben and I have to get back to the dance," I told them, eyeing the door. "You see, we're on the Decorations Committee. And a banner tore. And —"

"You can't get back," Seth said. His dark eyes narrowed on mine. "Mary told you the truth. You can't get back."

"That's stupid," Ben replied, shaking his head. "We're in the old building — right? We'll follow the hall till it leads to the new building. The gym is right downstairs."

Eloise coughed. I realized she was the one I'd heard when the lights were still out. She wiped her nose with a gray tissue. She appeared to have a cold.

"You're not in the old building," she said hoarsely.

"Then where are we?" Ben demanded. "The basement?"

The gray kids shook their heads.

"It's a little hard to explain," Seth said.

"Well, we'll find our way back," I told them, starting for the door. "I mean, the school isn't *that* big. We won't be lost for long."

"You're not really in the school," Eloise said, wiping her nose again.

"Excuse me?" Ben cried. "This looks a lot like a classroom to me. See? Desks? Chairs? Chalkboard?"

"Let's go," I said. I gave him a little push toward the door.

"Sit down," Seth ordered sharply.

Ben and I were nearly to the classroom door.

"I said sit down," Seth repeated.

"You'd better listen to him," the girl named Mona warned.

Seth motioned impatiently to two desks. "Sit."

I swallowed hard. I felt a chill of fear over my entire body. I didn't understand what was going on here. And I didn't really *want* to understand.

I just wanted to get away from this gray room and these black-and-white kids.

They moved across the room toward us. Their expressions were tense. Seth held his arms stiffly at his sides, as if ready for a fight.

"Sit down, guys," he insisted.

"Sorry. Some other time," Ben replied.

He and I both had the same idea in our heads.

We both turned and ran at the same time. We made a mad dash for the classroom door.

I got there first.

I grabbed the door handle. Turned it. And pulled.

"Come on! Come on!" Ben cried frantically.

"It — it won't open!" I shrieked.

The door was locked.

16

In a total panic, Ben grabbed the doorknob and bumped me out of the way. He tugged with both hands. Then he lowered his shoulder to the door and tried pushing it open.

But the door didn't budge.

"That door won't open," Seth said calmly.

I turned. Seth still held his arms tensely at his sides. The other four gray kids stood on either side of him, their eyes narrowed at us, squinting at us through the dim gray light.

"Why — why is it locked?" I stammered breathlessly.

"It isn't a door we can use," Mary replied. Another tear glistened on her pale gray cheek. "It leads to the world of color."

"Huh? Excuse me?" I cried.

"Whose idea is this little joke?" Ben demanded impatiently. "It's not funny, guys! Not funny!"

I could see that Ben was about to lose it. I put a hand on his arm, a signal to calm down.

64

I had a feeling that these kids weren't joking.

"How do we get out of here?" Ben demanded. He banged a fist against the door. "You can't keep us in this weird gray room. No way!"

Seth motioned to the desks again. "Sit down, guys," he pleaded again. "We're not trying to keep you here. And we don't plan to hurt you or anything."

Ben glanced at his watch. "But — but —"

"We'll try to explain," Mary offered. "You really should try to understand what has happened."

"Especially since you will be staying here with us," Eloise added.

Another cold shiver ran down my back. "Why do you keep saying that?" I asked.

They didn't reply.

Ben and I dropped into desk chairs. The three girls took chairs across from us. Eddie crossed his gray arms and leaned against the blackboard.

Seth pulled himself up onto the teacher's desk. "It's hard to know where to start," he said, running a hand back through his thick black hair.

"Start by telling us where we are," I demanded.

"And then tell us how to get to the gym," Ben insisted. "Make it short — okay?"

"You've come to the other side," Seth said.

Ben rolled his eyes. "The other side of *what*?" he asked impatiently.

"The other side of the wall," Seth replied.

Eloise sneezed. She pulled a wad of tissues from

the bag at her side. "I can't get rid of this cold," she sighed. "I think it's because there's no sunlight."

"No sunlight?" I cried. "The other side of the wall?" I let out a loud groan. "Will you all please stop talking in mysteries?"

Mona turned to Seth. "Start at the beginning," she said. "Maybe that will help them."

Eloise fumbled around in her gray bag. Finally, she pulled out a pack of tissues and placed them on the desk in front of her.

"Well, okay," Seth agreed. "The beginning."

Ben and I exchanged glances. Then we leaned forward to listen.

"The five of us were in the very first class at Bell Valley School," Seth began. "The school opened about fifty years ago, and —"

"Whoa! Wait a minute!" Ben jumped to his feet. "Tommy and I aren't morons!" he declared. "If you went to school fifty years ago, you'd be at least sixty years old!"

Seth nodded. "Guess you're good at math, huh?" It was a joke, but it sounded bitter.

"We haven't aged," Mary explained, straightening her black bangs with one hand. "We've stayed exactly the same age for fifty years!"

Ben rolled his eyes. "I think that elevator took us to Mars!" he whispered to me.

"It's all true," Eddie said, shifting his weight. "We're frozen here. Frozen in time."

"The elevator must move between your world and ours," Mona said, gazing back at it. "No one else has ever come here by elevator. It's not how we arrived."

"I don't understand," I confessed. "None of this makes sense to me. The elevator was boarded up. Hidden. Why did it bring us here?"

"It must be the only connection between our worlds," Mona said mysteriously.

"This is all crazy. We're missing the dance," Ben whispered.

"Let them finish the story," I told him. "Then we'll go."

Seth stood up and began pacing back and forth. "The first class at Bell Valley School was pretty small," he told us. "There were only twenty-five of us. It was a brand-new school, and we were kind of happy to be the first ones in it."

Eloise sneezed. Mona said, "Bless you."

"One day, our principal announced it was Class Photo Day," Seth continued. "A photographer came to take a group photo of our class."

"Was it a color photo?" Ben broke in. He laughed. But no one else did.

"School photos weren't in color in the nineteen forties," Mary told Ben. "They were in black and white."

"We all gathered in the library to take the photo," Seth continued. "All twenty-five of us. The photographer lined us up."

"I recognized him right away," Eddie broke in. "He was an angry man. An evil man. He hated kids."

"We were all in a crazy mood," Mona added. "We were laughing and joking around a lot and pretending to wrestle. And the photographer became furious because we wouldn't stand still for him."

"We all hated him," Eddie chimed in. "The whole town knew he was evil. But he was the only photographer around."

"I'll never forget his name," Eloise said sadly. "Mr. Chameleon. I'll never forget it. Because ... because a chameleon changes colors —and we can't."

"Mr. Chameleon?" Ben snickered. "Didn't he used to hang out with Mr. Lizard?"

"Ben, stop —" I pleaded.

I could see that Ben didn't believe a word of Seth's story. He kept making jokes. But Seth and the others looked so solemn, so bitter.

Staring at their old-fashioned clothes and haircuts, at their sad, gray faces, I believed them. They were the vanished kids, I realized. The lost class of 1947.

"The photographer lined us up in three rows," Seth continued, pacing back and forth, hands shoved in his gray pants pockets. "He stood behind his big box camera. It had a drape on the back that he stuck his head under. Then he raised the flash high.

"He told us to say 'cheese.' Then the flash went off with a loud *CRACK*."

"But it wasn't a normal flash," Mary broke in. "It was so bright ... so bright ..." Her voice trailed off.

"So bright, we couldn't see," Seth continued, shaking his head. "The room — the library — it disappeared in the flash. And when we could open our eyes, when we could see again ... we were here."

Ben opened his mouth. Probably to make another lame joke. But I guess he changed his mind. He closed his mouth without saying anything.

"We were here," Seth repeated, his voice shaking with emotion. He slammed the desk with his fist. "We weren't in the library anymore. We weren't in the real school anymore. We were here. Here in this black-and-white world."

"As if we were trapped inside a photograph," Mona broke in. "Trapped forever inside a black-and-white photograph."

"Trapped in Grayworld," Eddie said bitterly. "That's what we call it. Grayworld."

"We've tried everything," Eloise added. "We've tried every way to get back. We still call out for help. We still think maybe someone will come. . . ."

"I heard you," I murmured. "I was in class. And I heard you calling."

"But — but —" Ben sputtered. "I don't get it. Where exactly *are* we?"

No one answered for a long moment. Then Seth walked up to Ben. Pressing his hands on the desktop, he lowered his face close to Ben's, staring Ben in the eyes.

"Ben," he said, "did you ever see a wall and wonder what was on the other side?"

Ben glanced uncomfortably at me. "Yeah. I guess," he replied.

"Well, *we're* on the other side!" Seth cried. "*We're* on the other side of your world. And now, you are too."

"Soon you will be one of us!" Eddie said.

"No —!" Ben cried.

He said more, but I didn't hear him.

I glanced down at my hands — and opened my mouth in a high scream of horror.

17

"My — my *fingers*!" I shrieked.

I held both hands up to show them. My fingers had turned gray. The gray was spreading onto my palms.

Ben grabbed my hand and pulled it close to examine it. "Oh no," he murmured. "No . . ."

"Ben — yours too!" I cried.

He dropped my hand and studied his hands. His right hand was almost entirely gray. The fingers on his left hand were gray, and the color in his palm was starting to fade.

"No . . . no . . . ," he repeated, shaking his head.

I raised my eyes to the five gray kids. "You — you weren't joking," I choked out.

They stared back at us with blank expressions.

Mary stared at my hands. "It moves quickly," she said finally. "You'll see."

"No!" I cried, jumping to my feet. "What can we do? We can't turn gray! We *can't*!"

"You have no choice," Eloise said sadly. "You

are in Grayworld now. All color fades so quickly here."

"You are one of us now," Seth repeated. "Once you turn completely gray, you will never be able to turn back."

"No!" Ben and I both protested.

"We're getting out!" I cried. I kicked my chair aside and ran back to the classroom door. I turned the knob and struggled to pull it open.

Ben stepped up beside me, and we both pulled until we were groaning and our faces were bright red.

"It's bolted shut from the other side," Seth called. "You're wasting your time."

"No —" I insisted. "We're getting out. We're getting out *now*!"

With a desperate cry, I raised both fists and started pounding on the wall. "Help us!" I screamed. "Somebody — help us! Can you hear me? Please — help!"

I pounded until my fists hurt. Then I lowered my hands with a sigh.

"Don't you think we already tried that?" Mary asked bitterly. "We pound on the walls and call for help all the time."

"But no one ever answers," Eloise added. "And no one ever comes to help."

I gazed down at my hands. They were completely gray to the wrists. I pulled up my sleeves. The color of my arms was starting to fade.

"Ben — !" I started. He was staring at his graying skin too.

My mind whirred. I suddenly felt dizzy.

"How do we escape from here? How do we get back to our world?"

"Maybe the elevator?" Ben suggested.

"It's no use," Seth warned.

But we ignored him and bolted through the aisle between the desks. To the alcove in back of the big gray classroom. The narrow alcove that held the elevator.

"There's no elevator button," Mary called after us. "No way to call the elevator."

"It never runs," Seth added. "It hasn't run in fifty years. When we heard it moving tonight, we couldn't believe it."

"There's *got* to be a way!" I cried.

I smoothed my hand over the wall beside the elevator doors. "There's got to be a hidden button." The wall felt warm and smooth.

I pounded it with my fist until my whole hand ached.

Ben pressed his hands along the crack between the two doors. With a groan, he struggled to pry the elevator doors open.

No luck.

"A screwdriver?" he called over his shoulder. "Does anyone have a screwdriver?"

"Or maybe a knife, or a stick, or something?" I added. "To pry the doors apart?"

"We tried it," Eloise moaned in her hoarse, scratchy voice. "We tried everything. *Everything!*"

I kicked the metal doors hard. I felt so frustrated, and angry, and frightened — all at the same time.

Pain shot up my foot and leg. I hobbled back against the wall, breathing hard.

My shirtsleeves were graying. I pulled up one sleeve. The gray on my skin had moved past my wrist.

"Sit down with us," Mary called. "Sit down and wait. It really isn't that bad."

"You get used to it," Seth added softly.

"Used to it?" I cried shrilly, still breathing hard. "Used to a world without any color? Used to being totally in black and white? And not being able to go home? Or go anywhere?"

Mary lowered her head. The others gazed back at Ben and me, their gray faces solemn and sad.

"I — I'm not going to get used to it!" I stammered. "Ben and I are getting out of here."

I raised one hand and rubbed it with the other. I guess I thought maybe I could rub the gray off. My skin felt warm and soft as ever. It didn't *feel* any different.

But the color was gone. And the gray was creeping up, creeping up fast.

"What are we going to do?" Ben cried. His eyes were wild. His voice came out high and shrill.

"The window!" I shouted, pointing. "Come on. Out the window!"

"No!" Seth shouted. He moved quickly to block our path. "No — don't! I'm warning you —"

"Don't go out there!" Eddie cried.

Why are they trying to stop us? I wondered. They don't want us to escape! They want to keep us here! They want us to be as gray as they are!

"Out of the way, Seth!" I cried.

Ben dodged one way. I dodged the other.

Seth made a grab for me. But I slid away from him.

And dove to the window ledge.

Staring out into the gray night, I shoved up the window.

"Stay away from the kids!"

"They're crazy! They've all gone crazy!"

"They'll take you to the pit!"

We heard their cries and warnings behind us. But they didn't make any sense to us. So we ignored them.

Ben and I climbed onto the window ledge — and scrambled out.

18

Ben dropped onto the ground with a hard *THUD*. I followed him, landing on my feet on soft grass.

The night sky spread overhead, a solid black. No stars. No moon.

Seth and the others appeared at the window, shouting and signaling for us to come back. But we both took off, jogging over the dark grass.

We crossed the street and saw low, dark houses set far back on gray lawns. No lights shone in the windows. No cars came by. No one was out walking.

"Is this Bell Valley?" Ben asked as we crossed another street and kept jogging. "Why doesn't it look familiar?"

"These aren't the same houses across from the school," I said.

A chill of fear made me stop running.

How could there be a whole different town out here? And where were the people who lived here?

Was it deserted? Was it like a movie set? I suddenly wondered. Not a real neighborhood at all?

The kids' warnings repeated in my ears. Maybe Ben and I made a mistake, I thought. Maybe we should have listened to them.

I turned back toward the school. Wisps of fog came floating up from the ground. The school rose darkly behind the spreading gray mist.

Startled, I squinted hard at it. "Whoa — Ben," I gasped. "Check out the school."

He was studying it too. "That's not our school!" he exclaimed.

We were staring at a low, square building with a flat roof. Only one story high. Gray light flooded from the only window facing the street.

The light fell on a slender, bare flagpole planted near the street. And a small set of swings, silvery gray in the dim wash of light.

"We're in a different world," I said, my voice shaky and shrill. "We're in a different world — so close to ours."

"But — but —" Ben sputtered.

The clumps of fog began to float together, forming a billowing wall. It moved quickly up from the ground, hiding the bottom of the building from us now.

"Let's keep going," I urged Ben. "There's *got* to be a way out of here!"

We started to jog again, moving past darkened

houses and empty lots. Running under black-trunked trees, all winter bare. Our shoes clattering over streets without cars or streetlights.

I kept gazing up at the sky, hoping to see the moon or the blinking light of a star. But I stared up at a ceiling of solid black.

We're like shadows, I thought. Shadows running through shadows.

Stop it, Tommy! I scolded myself. Don't start thinking weird thoughts. Just keep your mind straight ahead on what you have to do.

Which is to find a way to escape from this place.

We jogged past a black mailbox, across another empty street. And as we ran, the fog swept around us.

It floated low at first, clinging to the dark grass, billowing over the streets. There was no breeze. No wind at all.

But the fog quickly began to rise. It rose all around us. Hiding the houses behind it. Hiding the bare trees and streets and driveways — hiding *everything* behind a thick, swirling curtain of gray.

With a groan, Ben stopped jogging.

I ran right into him. "Hey — !" I cried out breathlessly. "Why did you stop?"

"I can't see anything," he choked out. "The fog . . ." He lowered his hands to his knees and leaned forward, struggling to catch his breath.

"We're not getting anywhere — are we?" I asked softly. "I mean, we could probably keep running forever. And we'd never get out of this place."

"Maybe we should wait till morning," Ben suggested, still bent over. "Then the fog will probably be gone and we can see where we're going."

"Maybe . . . ," I said doubtfully.

I shivered. I wondered how much of me had turned gray. Did I have any color left?

I pulled up my shirt and struggled to see. But it was too dark. Everything looked black and gray. I couldn't tell.

"What do you want to do?" I asked Ben. "Go back to the school?"

The fog swept around us. So thick, I could barely see him.

"I — I don't think we could find the school in this fog," he stammered. I could hear the fear in his voice.

I turned back.

He was right. I couldn't see the street or the trees on the other side of the thick mist.

"Maybe we can retrace our steps," I suggested. "If we keep going in that direction —" I pointed.

But in the thick, spinning fog, I wasn't sure it was the right direction.

"This was dumb," Ben muttered. "We should have listened to those kids. They were trying to help us, and —"

"It's too late to think about that," I said sharply. "I have an idea. Let's try to find our way through the fog to one of the houses and spend the night there."

"You mean break in?" Ben demanded.

"They seem to be empty," I replied. The fog swirled thicker, wrapping us up tightly. I tugged his arm. "Come on. We'll find a place to wait until morning. It's better than standing out here all night."

"I guess . . ." he agreed.

We turned and began walking up a sloping front yard. We had to move slowly because we could barely see.

We took six or seven steps — and then I let out a scream as someone knocked me to the ground.

19

"Ohhhhhh!" A terrified moan escaped my throat.

I rolled onto my back.

A black cat tumbled beside me.

A cat?

It had jumped onto my shoulders from a tree limb.

The cat stared up at me with gray eyes. Its black fur bristled. Its tail stood straight up.

And then it took off, vanishing into the fog.

I pulled myself shakily to my feet.

"Tommy, what happened?" Ben demanded.

"Didn't you see that cat?" I cried. "It jumped down on me. Knocked me to the ground. I thought . . . I thought . . ." The words caught in my throat.

"Are you okay? I couldn't see it," Ben replied. "The fog — it's so thick. All of a sudden, you screamed. You scared me to death!"

I rubbed the back of my neck. Why did the cat jump on me like that? I wondered.

Maybe it's lonely, I decided. With no other people around.

And just as I thought that, I heard a girl's voice. "Over here!" she called.

And then a boy, very nearby, shouted: "Don't let them get away! Grab them!"

20

Ben and I squinted into the fog. We heard shrill voices. And then the thump of footsteps over the grass. But we couldn't see anyone.

We didn't know which way to run.

"This way! Over here!" the girl repeated breathlessly to her friend.

"Stop them!" another girl chimed in.

Ben and I spun around. "Who's there?" I tried to shout. But my voice spilled out weak and frightened. "Who is it?"

And then, figures appeared in the swirling fog. Shadowy, gray figures. Running toward us and then stopping just near enough to see through the curtain of gray.

Staring, surprised faces.

Their arms out. Bodies tense. Hair blowing in the circling mist.

I backed up to Ben. We stood back to back, gaping out at them as they formed a tight circle around us.

"They're — kids!" Ben exclaimed. "More kids!"

Are they the rest of the missing class? I wondered.

"Hey —!" I called to them. "What are you doing out here?"

They stared back at us in silence.

The fog billowed and shifted. I saw a short, black-haired girl whispering to a big kid in an old-fashioned-looking black jacket. And then the fog covered them again, and they seemed to vanish before my eyes.

Other kids appeared and disappeared. There must have been about twenty of them.

They spoke softly to one another, gazing out at us, keeping in a tight circle.

"What are you doing out here?" I repeated, trying not to sound as frightened as I felt. "My friend and I — we're lost. Can you help us?"

"You still have color," a girl murmured.

"Color. Color. Color." The word was repeated among the circle of gray kids.

"They must be the other kids from the class," Ben whispered. "The kids Seth and the others warned us about."

Seth's warning flashed back into my mind: *They're crazy. They've all gone crazy.*

"We're lost!" I cried. "Can you help us?"

They didn't reply. They whispered excitedly among themselves.

"*Turn, turn,*" a boy called suddenly. So loud, I jumped back.

"What did you say?" I demanded. "Can you help us?"

"*Turn, turn,*" a girl repeated.

"We don't belong here!" Ben cried. "We're trying to get away from here. But we're totally lost."

"*Turn, turn,*" a few voices murmured.

"Please — answer us!" I begged. "Can you help us?"

And then they all chanted, "*Turn, turn.*" And they began to dance.

Keeping the circle tight, they moved to the right in a rapid rhythm. They raised one leg high, and stepped to the right. Lowered the leg and gave a little kick. Then another high step to the right.

Some kind of weird dance.

"*Turn, turn,*" they chanted. "*Turn, turn.*"

"Please — stop!" Ben and I both pleaded. "Why are you doing that? Are you trying to scare us?"

"*Turn, turn.*" The dark, dancing figures moved in and out of the swirling fog.

The fog lifted for a moment, and I saw that they were holding hands as they danced. Holding hands tightly. Keeping the circle closed.

Keeping Ben and me inside.

"*Turn, turn,*" they chanted. A step, then a kick. "*Turn, turn.*"

"What are they doing?" Ben whispered to me. "Is it a game or something?"

I swallowed hard. "I don't think so," I replied.

The fog shifted again. It lowered over the grass, then billowed away.

I squinted at the chanting faces as they moved in the circle.

Their expressions were hard.

Their eyes cold.

Cold, unfriendly faces.

"Turn, turn. Turn, turn."

"Stop it!" I screamed. "Give us a break! What are you doing? Please — somebody explain!"

"Turn, turn." The chant continued. The circle of kids moved to the right. They stared at Ben and me, as if challenging us — as if daring us to stop them.

"Turn, turn.
Turn to gray.
Turn, turn.
Turn to gray!"

The circle spun around us. The kids danced in rhythm in the billowing fog. A steady, frightening rhythm.

So cold . . . so menacing.

So *crazy*!

"Turn, turn.
Turn to gray.
Turn, turn.
Turn to gray."

And suddenly, watching the eerie dance, listening to their machinelike chant, I knew.

I knew what they were doing.

It was some kind of weird ceremony.

They were watching us, holding us there.

Holding us there until we were gray like them.

21

"Turn, turn.

Turn to gray."

As the kids moved in their tight circle, chanting softly, I studied their faces. So hard . . . so cold.

They were trying to frighten us.

I counted nine girls and ten boys. All dressed in old-fashioned clothes. Big, heavy shoes. And I suddenly wished this was all an old movie. All just a movie and not really happening to Ben and me.

"Turn, turn.

Turn to gray."

"Why are you doing this?" Ben shouted over their eerie chant. "Why won't you talk to us?"

They continued their circle dance, ignoring his cries.

I turned to him, leaning close so that he could hear me. "We have to make a run for it," I said. "They're crazy. They're going to keep us here. Until we are totally gray like them."

Ben nodded solemnly, his eyes on the circle of kids.

He cupped his hands around his mouth to reply to me. And I gasped. His hands were completely gray.

I raised both of my hands to my face. Gray. Solid gray.

How far had the gray traveled? How much time did Ben and I have?

"We've *got* to get away from them," I told him. "Come on, Ben. On the count of three. You run this way. And I'll run that way." I motioned in two different directions.

"If we take them by surprise, maybe we can break through," I said.

"And then what?" Ben replied.

I didn't want to answer that question. I didn't *know* the answer. "Let's just get away from them!" I cried. "I can't stand that stupid chanting for one more second!"

Ben nodded. He sucked in a deep breath.

"One . . . " I counted.

"Turn, turn.

Turn to gray."

The chanting kids had tightened their circle. They were nearly arm in arm.

Had they read our minds?

"Two . . . " I counted. I tensed my leg muscles. Prepared to run.

The curtain of fog had lifted. Puffs of mist clung to the ground. But I could see dark houses beyond the circle of kids.

If we can break through their linked arms, maybe we can hide in one of those houses, I thought.

"Good luck," Ben murmured.

"Three!" I shouted.

We lowered our heads and started to run.

22

I went about four steps and slipped on the wet grass.

"OW!" I cried out as pain shot up my right leg. Did I pull a muscle?

The chanting stopped. The gray kids let out shouts of surprise.

My leg throbbed with pain. I had to stop. I bent to rub the leg muscle.

Raising my gaze, I saw Ben dart toward the circle. "Aaaiiiii!" He let out a wild scream as he ran.

Two boys tackled him: one high, one low. Ben dropped to the grass, and they fell on top of him.

"Get off! Get off me!" Ben shrieked.

A boy and girl grabbed me roughly. They spun me around. And shoved me hard toward Ben.

"Let us go!" I cried. "What are you doing? Why are you keeping us here?"

They pulled Ben to his feet. And shoved us together.

They grouped around us quickly, bodies tensed, ready to capture us if we tried another escape.

"We're not going anywhere," I sighed. "Will somebody *please* explain what is going on here."

"*Turn, turn,*" a girl with long gray braids said in a husky voice.

"I've *heard* that!" I cried angrily.

"*Turn to gray,*" the girl added. "We're waiting for you to turn."

"Why?" I demanded. "Just tell us why."

"No color in the moon," she replied. "No color in the stars."

"No color in my dreams," a boy added sadly.

"Please — make sense!" Ben pleaded. "I — I don't understand!"

I rubbed my sore leg. The pain had faded, but the muscle still ached.

"Just help us get back to the school," I pleaded.

"We left the school!" a boy shouted. "No color in the school."

"No color anywhere," a girl cried. "We'll never go back to school."

"No school! No school! No school!" some kids chanted.

"But we have to get back there!" I insisted.

"No school! No school! No school!" they chanted again.

"It's no use," Ben whispered in my ear. "They're totally messed up! They don't make any sense at all."

I felt a chill. The air was turning colder.

A wave of terror swept over me. I struggled to fight it back.

Kids grabbed Ben and me. They pushed us roughly across the grass. They held us tightly by the shoulders and forced us forward.

"Where are you taking us?" I screamed.

They didn't answer.

Ben and I struggled to break free. But there were too many of them. And they were too strong.

They pushed us up a dark hill. Wisps of fog swirled around our feet as we climbed. The tall grass was wet and slippery.

"Where are we going?" I cried. "Tell us! Where are you taking us?"

"The Black Pit!" a girl exclaimed. She pressed her mouth close to my ear as we walked. "Will you jump, or will we have to push you?"

23

"Pit? What kind of pit?" I screamed.

No one answered.

We stopped at the top of the hill. They kept their tight grip on Ben and me. Over Ben's shoulder, I saw four kids approaching. As they came nearer, I saw that they were carrying four large buckets.

They set the buckets down in a row. They shoved Ben and me toward them.

Steam poured up from a dark, bubbling liquid inside. A sharp, sour aroma rose up in the steam.

A girl carried a stack of metal cups in her arms. She handed a cup to a boy. He dipped it into the thick black liquid. It made a hissing sound as the cup dipped low into the liquid.

"Ohhh!" I gasped as the boy raised the steaming cup to his lips, tilted his head back, and poured the disgusting liquid down his throat.

"No color in the cup!" a boy shouted.

"Drink the blackness!" a girl cried.

"Drink! Drink! Drink!" Kids cheered and applauded.

They lined up eagerly. And as Ben and I stared in horror, they each dipped a cup into the smelly black gunk — and then drank it down.

"No color in the drink! No color in the cup!"

"Drink! Drink the blackness!"

I tried once again to break free. But three boys held me now. I couldn't move.

Kids were cheering and laughing. A boy drank a whole cup of the smelly black liquid — and then spewed it into the air.

Loud cheers.

A girl spit loudly and sprayed black gunk into the face of the girl beside her. A boy sprayed the black liquid up like a fountain.

"We cover ourselves in blackness!" a boy boomed in a loud, deep voice. "We cover ourselves because there's no color in the moon! No color in the stars! No color on the earth!"

A girl spit black gunk over the hair of a short boy with glasses. The black liquid rolled slowly down his forehead and over his glasses. He bent to fill his cup, drank, and spit a gob of it down the front of the girl's coat.

Laughing and cheering, hooting at the top of their lungs, they sprayed each other. Spit and sprayed the hot black gunk until they were all drenched, all dripping, covered in oily blackness.

"No color in the cup! No color in the drink!"

And then the hands gripped me tighter. And Ben and I were pulled to the top of the hill.

I gazed down the other side. And saw a steep drop. And down below, at the bottom . . .

Too dark.

I couldn't see a thing. But I could hear the loud bubbling. I could see thick steam floating up, wave after wave of it. And I could smell the sharp, sour odor — so strong, I started to gag.

"The Black Pit!" someone cried. "Into the Black Pit!"

Lots of kids cheered.

Ben and I were pushed to the edge of the drop-off.

"Jump! Jump! Jump!" some kids began to chant. "Jump into the Black Pit!"

"But — why?" I shrieked. "Why are you doing this?"

"Cover yourself in blackness!" a girl screamed. "Cover yourself like us!"

Kids laughed and cheered.

Ben turned to me, his face twisted in fear. "It — it's boiling hot down there," he stammered, gazing into the bubbling pit below. "And it smells like dead animals!"

"Jump! Jump! Jump!" kids began to chant.

My eyes swept over them. Laughing. Cheering. The black goo running down their faces, down their clothes. The kids tossed their heads back and spewed gobs of black liquid into the air.

"Jump! Jump! Jump!"

Suddenly, the chanting and laughter stopped.

I heard screams.

Strong hands grabbed me around the waist from behind.

And shoved me hard — into the steaming pit.

24

No.

I didn't fall. I didn't go over the side.

The hands held on to me. Spun me around.

I squinted into a familiar face. Seth!

"Run!" he cried. "We came to rescue you!"

I turned and saw Mary and Eloise guiding Ben down the hill.

"Let's go!" Seth cried.

We started to run. But we didn't get far.

The other kids had been startled at first. But they quickly got over their surprise. And formed a tight circle around us.

"They've trapped us!" I cried. "How can we break through?"

We stopped and stared at them as they began to circle us, moving silently, their faces smeared with the black liquid, their clothing drenched and stained.

"I thought we could outrun them," Seth started. "But —"

I lowered my gaze to a pile of dead leaves on the ground. And an idea flashed into my mind.

I shoved my hand into the pocket of my khakis.

"Get ready," I warned the others.

Ben turned to me. "Get ready for what?" he demanded.

"Get ready," I repeated. "Get ready to move."

25

"Okay!" I cried.

I raised the lighter. Clicked it once. Twice.

A yellow flame shot up.

"Owww!" a girl cried.

Several other kids cried out. Some shielded their eyes or turned away from the flame.

"Too bright!" a girl screamed.

"My eyes! It hurts my eyes!"

"Grab it! Grab it!" a boy wailed.

But I wasn't finished.

I lowered the flame to the pile of leaves at our feet. The leaves caught instantly, with a loud *WHOOOOSH*. Bright orange flames roared up.

"Nooooo!" The kids covered their eyes and cried out in pain.

"Let's go!" I called to Ben and the others. But I didn't need to say it. They were already running over the dark grass. I lowered my head and ran after them.

I heard kids screaming and crying behind us.

"I can't see! I can't see!"

"Somebody — do something!"

"Put out the fire!"

I glanced back. The pile of burning leaves sent up a darting wall of red-orange light. So bright against the black night sky.

Covering their eyes, the kids were scrambling away, running in all directions. No one was chasing after us.

Trotting hard through the foggy night, Seth and the two girls led us away from the hill. "We tried to warn you about the others," Mary said breathlessly. "But you ran away. You wouldn't listen."

"They've lost their minds," Seth added sadly. "They can't think straight anymore."

"They're like some kind of wild gang now," Eloise added. "They have their own laws. Their own strange traditions. They cover themselves in black goo every night. It's — it's really frightening."

"That's why the five of us stay in the school," Eloise explained. "We're afraid of them too."

"They do horrible, crazy things," Mary said. "They've given up all hope. They don't care what they do."

I shivered. The gray moon had disappeared behind clouds again, and the air grew cold. The three gray kids seemed to fade with the moonlight.

I heard shouts. From nearby. Excited voices.

"They're coming back!" I cried.

101

"We'd better hurry," Seth said. "Follow us."

He and the two girls turned and began running toward the street. Ben and I followed, keeping in the deep shadow of the tall hedges that lined the yards.

I heard the shouts again, from close behind us.

"Where are you taking us?" Ben asked in a breathless whisper.

"Back to the school," Seth replied.

"To help us get out of this place?" I cried. "To help us back to our own world?"

"No," Seth replied without slowing his stride. "We told you, Tommy. We can't help you go back. But you'll be safer in the school with us."

"A lot safer," Mary added.

Jogging hard, Ben and I followed them through dark yards and over empty streets. The bare trees cracked and groaned overhead. The only other sound was the steady *THUD* of our shoes as we ran.

I didn't hear the other kids' voices. But I knew they had to be nearby. Still searching for us.

I breathed a sigh of relief when the little school building came into view. Ben and I hurried inside. We followed Seth and the two girls back to the large classroom. Mona and Eddie were waiting there for us.

I sat down at a desk and struggled to catch my breath. When I looked up, I found all five kids staring wide-eyed at Ben and me.

"What's wrong?" I demanded.

They didn't answer for a long moment. Then, finally, Eloise said, "You'd better check yourself out in the mirror." She pointed to a tall mirror near the elevator alcove.

Ben and I made our way quickly to the mirror.

My heart was pounding by the time I stepped in front of it. A heavy feeling of dread swept over me.

I knew what I was about to see.

But I prayed I was wrong.

I took a deep breath — and gazed into the mirror.

26

"Nooooo." Ben opened his mouth in a sorrowful moan.

We stared at two gray figures.

My khakis, my shirt. Gray now. My hair. My eyes. All of me. All in shades of gray.

"We're almost one of them," Ben murmured. He uttered another moan. "What are the school colors here? Gray and gray?" He tried to laugh. But I saw his whole body tremble.

"No — wait!" I cried. "Ben, look. We still have a little time!"

I pointed into the mirror.

My ears were gray. And the gray had spread over my lips and chin. But my cheeks still held their color. My cheeks and my nose.

Ben's face was the same. "That's all that's left," he sighed. "The front of my face."

"We're sorry," Mary said, stepping up behind us. "We're really sorry. In a few minutes, you'll be gray like us."

"No —!" I insisted, spinning away from the mirror. "There's got to be a way. Hasn't *anyone* ever escaped?"

Seth's answer shocked me.

"Yes," he said softly. "One girl escaped from Grayworld. Just a few weeks ago."

"After fifty years, one of us made it back to the world," Mona sighed.

"How?" Ben and I cried at the same time.

"How did she do it?" I demanded.

They all shook their heads. "We don't know," Eloise replied sadly. "She just disappeared. We've been waiting for her to come back for us."

"When the elevator opened tonight, we thought it was her," Eddie said. "We thought she had come back to rescue us."

Greta!

Her face flashed into my mind.

Of course! Greta, that strange girl with her gray eyes, her white-blond hair, her all-black outfits.

Greta had escaped from Grayworld. Greta had returned to the world of color. No wonder she was so eager to get her hands on Thalia's bright lipstick!

Greta . . .

Why *hadn't* she returned to rescue her friends?

How did she make her escape?

My eyes traveled to the elevator at the back of the room. *Open!* I ordered it silently. *Open up — now! Please open!*

But, of course, the gray doors remained shut.

I shoved my hands into my khakis pockets. Thinking hard, trying to fight down my panic, I started to walk to the front of the room.

Ben slumped into a chair, shaking his head sadly. "This can't be happening," he muttered. He pounded the desktop angrily. "This can't be happening!"

"Think, Tommy. Think," I instructed myself out loud. "There's got to be a way to stop the gray. There's got to be a way to bring the color back. Think!"

My mind raced. I was too frightened to think clearly.

Every muscle in my body tensed.

Thinking hard, I pulled out the plastic lighter from my pocket. Nervously, I twirled it between my fingers. Slid it from hand to hand.

Think! *Think!*

I fumbled with the lighter. It fell out of my hand and clattered onto the floor.

I stared at it as I bent to pick it up. The lighter had been bright red. But now the plastic had faded to gray.

But the flame . . .

Suddenly, I had an idea.

I stood up and turned to the others. I raised the lighter. "What if . . . " I started, thinking hard. Excited by my flash of hope.

"What if I lit up the room with yellow light from

the other world? Do you think the color — the yellow light — would wash away the gray?"

"You already tried it — outside," Ben reminded me.

"But that was outside," I replied. "What if I light it near the wall? Do you think the bright color will make the gray wall fade away so that we can escape to the other side, the side of color?"

They stared back at me, their eyes locked on the lighter in my hand.

I didn't wait for their reply.

"I'm going to try it," I announced.

I raised the plastic lighter high.

Their eyes followed the lighter as I raised it high.

"Good luck," Ben whispered. "Good luck to us all."

I clicked the lighter.

Clicked it again.

Clicked it.

Clicked it hard.

It wouldn't light.

27

I slammed the lighter onto the desktop.

"It's out!" I wailed. "I used it up. It's out of fluid."

"No —" Ben cried. "Try it again, Tommy. Please — give it one more try."

I groaned and picked up the lighter. My hand was trembling. My throat suddenly felt so dry.

It seemed like such a good idea. If only I could get it to flame.

"Here goes," I murmured, raising the lighter again. "One more try."

My palm slippery from sweat, I nearly dropped the lighter again. I tightened my grip on it. Raised my thumb.

Clicked it.

Clicked it again, harder.

And the flame shot up.

"Yesssss!" Ben cried.

But his happy cry faded quickly.

The flame leaping up from the lighter was gray.

Everyone groaned.

I stared at the gray flame, dancing on top of the gray lighter. Held tight in my gray fist. "It's no use," I choked out.

I clicked off the flame and shoved the lighter back into my pocket. I turned to Ben. "Sorry," I muttered glumly. "I tried."

Ben nodded, swallowing hard.

I gasped. "Ben — your face! Your cheeks!"

"Gray?" he asked softly.

I nodded. "Your nose is all that's left," I told him. "Your nose has the only color."

"Yours too," he reported.

The five gray kids stood in silence across the room. Seth shook his head sadly.

What could they say?

This had already happened to them. They had lived in a black-and-white world for fifty years.

And now Ben and I were doomed to be part of that cold, gloomy world.

I rubbed my nose. How long would it keep its color? I wondered.

How long until I became one of them?

My eyes wandered to the elevator. If only Ben and I had taken the *stairs* to the art room. If only . . .

Too late to think about that now.

I stared hard at the elevator doors. Once again, I silently ordered them to open.

I let out a startled cry when I heard a loud, rumbling sound.

Everyone jumped up. Alert. Listening.

The rumble grew to a roar. "What's happening?" Ben cried.

"The elevator!" Eloise gasped, pointing.

We all hurried across the room. We were just a few feet away — when the elevator doors slid open.

We all stepped up to see who was inside.

"Greta!" I cried.

28

No. Not Greta.

To my shock, *Thalia* stood in the elevator doorway.

She peered out tensely. Her blond hair gleamed in the elevator light. Her blue dress sparkled brightly. The color almost hurt my eyes.

A red-lipped smile spread over her face. "I found you! I *did* it!" she cried happily.

She came running out of the elevator. With a happy cry, she threw her arms around Mary and hugged her tight. Then she hugged Eloise and Seth, Mona and Eddie.

Happy cries rang out from everyone.

"Thalia — you came back!"

"Are you okay?"

"We've been waiting for you!"

"Whoa — wait — the elevator!" I cried. "Don't let it go!"

I made a frantic dive.

Too late.

The doors slid shut.

I crashed into them and bounced off. "Nooooo!" I let out a long, frantic wail. "Nooooooo! The elevator! The elevator!" I banged on the doors with both fists.

I spun around to face Thalia.

She gasped and raised a hand to her mouth. "Oh — I'm so sorry!" she cried. Her blue eyes grew wide. "I — I was so happy to see my friends, I forgot!"

"But — but —" I sputtered.

Trembling, I slumped against the wall. Our one chance to escape. Too late . . . too late . . .

The five gray kids circled around Thalia, hugging her, laughing, asking her a thousand questions.

"We missed you so much!" Eloise cried. "We waited for you to come back and rescue us."

"I missed you guys too," Thalia told them. "I tried to come back. But I couldn't find the way. I didn't know how to get back here — until tonight."

She turned to Ben and me. "I escaped a few weeks ago," she explained. "Just before school started. I went over to your world, the real world. But I had to disguise myself."

"You mean —" I started.

"The makeup," Thalia continued. "The makeup and the lipstick. I had to keep putting that stuff on all the time. To cover up my gray skin. I —"

"But your eyes —" I interrupted. "They're blue."

"Contact lenses," she explained. She let out a long sigh. "It was so hard, so much work. I had to be so careful. I had to apply coat after coat of makeup and lipstick. I couldn't let anyone know.

"Kids made fun of me," Thalia sighed. "But that wasn't the worst part. I wanted to stay in the world of color and brightness. But I was a fake. A phony, covering up with makeup. I no longer belonged there. I belonged here in Grayworld."

Thalia sighed again. "But I couldn't find the way back. Then tonight, you and Ben didn't return to the gym. I went searching for you. I found the hole in the boarded-up wall. And I found the elevator. And it brought me here, to my friends."

"Welcome back," Mary said, putting a gray arm around the shoulders of Thalia's dress. The color on the dress had already started to fade.

"You're right. This is where you belong," Seth told her.

"When you escaped, we thought about you all the time," Mona added. "We wondered how you were doing. And we wondered if you would come back for us."

"You don't want to go there," Thalia replied. "And I don't want to go back. We don't belong there. We cannot live there. I don't want to pretend anymore. I just want to stay here with you and be myself."

She pulled a makeup kit and a tube of lipstick from her bag and tossed it down on a desktop. "No more makeup. No more lipstick. No more pretending."

"But what about *us*?" Ben cried. "Tommy and I have only a minute or two more before we're totally gray!"

"Aren't you going to help us escape from here?" I pleaded. "Aren't you going to help us get back?"

Thalia shook her head sadly. "I'm sorry, guys."

29

I swallowed hard, thinking about home. My dad. My new mom. My dog.

I'll never see them again, I realized.

I'll never see *color* again. Never see blue ocean waves or a red, setting sun.

"I'm sorry, guys," Thalia repeated. "Sorry I didn't explain this to you right away."

"Explain what?" I cried.

"I think I can get you back to the other side," she said.

She picked up her lipstick tube. "This is how I escaped a few weeks ago," she said. "This lipstick tube was buried in my bag for fifty years. I'd forgotten all about it."

She unscrewed the cap and showed us the bright red lipstick. "I found it a few weeks ago. When I opened it, it was still red!" Thalia exclaimed. "It was some kind of miracle. Maybe because it had been closed up. It still had its color."

Thalia moved to the wall. "I was so excited to see the color red after fifty years," she explained. "I started drawing on the wall with it. And to my shock, wherever I spread the lipstick, it made a hole in the wall!"

"That's amazing!" Eddie cried.

The others excitedly agreed.

"The lipstick burned right through the wall," Thalia continued. "I — I was so shocked, I didn't know what to do. I drew a window on the wall. And I climbed through it. I escaped. That's how I did it."

She raised the lipstick tube to the gray wall. "I tried to come back for you guys," she told her friends. "But the hole closed up as soon as I went through it."

She frowned. "I drew a lipstick window on the wall on the other side. But in the real world, lipstick is only lipstick. It didn't work. I couldn't get back to you. I had no way of finding you, no way to return here."

I glanced at Ben. To my horror, he had turned completely gray. Except . . . except for the tip of his nose.

"Thalia — hurry!" I begged. "Draw a window for Ben and me! Please — we don't have any time left!"

Without another word, she turned to the wall.

Her hand moved quickly, outlining a red window. Filling it in.

"Hurry! Please, hurry!" I pleaded, staring as she frantically rubbed the red lipstick over the wall.

Would it work?

30

As soon as she finished the window, I grabbed Ben. I shoved him through the hole. "Come on!" I cried. "We can do it!"

"Good-bye, Ben. Good-bye, Tommy," the others called.

Halfway through the wall, I turned back to them. "Come with us!" I cried. "Hurry! You can come with us!"

"No, we can't," Seth called sadly.

"Thalia is right. We'd hate it. We belong here now," Mary said.

"Don't forget me!" Thalia called. Her voice broke with sadness. She turned away.

I turned too. Turned to the other world, *our* world. Ben and I stepped through the wall. And found ourselves back in school.

I heard music booming down the hall. Kids shouting and laughing.

The dance!

We were back at the dance.

With a gleeful shout, I shoved open the door to the boys' room. Ben and I dove inside. Ran up to the mirror.

Gaped at ourselves.

Our colorful selves.

All red and blue and pink and yellow. All in color! So many colors!

We slapped each other high fives. And tossed back our heads and screamed out our happiness. Screamed and screamed.

We were back. Back to normal. Back in the world.

Back at the dance.

We banged open the boys' room door. Burst into the hall.

And ran into Mrs. Borden.

"*There* you are!" she cried. "I've been looking all over for you two!"

She grabbed each of us by the hand and began tugging us down the hall.

"Mrs. Borden — we have to tell you —" I started.

"Later," she interrupted. She pushed us into the gym. "We've all been waiting for you. You've held everyone up."

"But — you don't *understand*!" I sputtered.

"You want to be in the photo — don't you?" Mrs. Borden demanded. Kids were lined up in front of the bleachers. She shoved Ben and me into the front row.

"We want everyone who worked on the dance in the photo," Mrs. Borden declared.

She turned to the photographer behind his camera. "Okay, Mr. Chameleon," she called. "You can take the shot now!"

"Mr. *who*?" I cried. "No! Wait! *Wait!*"

FLASH.

About R.L. Stine

R.L. Stine is the most popular author in America. He is the creator of the *Goosebumps*, *Give Yourself Goosebumps*, *Fear Street*, and *Ghosts of Fear Street* series, among other popular books. He has written more than 100 scary novels for kids. Bob lives in New York City with his wife, Jane, teenage son, Matt, and dog, Nadine.

Add *more*

Goosebumps ®

to your collection . . .
A chilling preview of
what's next from
R.L. STINE

WEREWOLF SKIN

14

"They saw *you*, Alex," my aunt said. "They saw you prowling around their house late last night. They are *very* angry about it."

She poured herself a mug of coffee and came over to the table. She sat down and swept a strand of gray hair off her forehead.

"What were you doing outside last night?" my uncle asked.

"I'm really sorry. But I had no choice. I left my camera out in the woods," I explained. "I had to run out and get it. I couldn't leave it out all night — especially with the rain."

"But you didn't have to go near the Marlings' house — did you?" Aunt Marta demanded.

"I — I heard animal howls from inside their house!" I blurted out. "And I saw strange footprints going up to the bedroom window at the side."

Uncle Colin nodded calmly. He took a long sip

of coffee. "The footprints were probably from their dogs," he said, glancing at Aunt Marta.

"Dogs?" I cried.

They both nodded. "They have two huge German shepherds," my aunt explained. "Mean as they come."

"And as big as wolves," Uncle Colin added, shaking his head. He reached for a slice of toast and began to butter it.

I sighed. I felt a little better.

Two German shepherds. That explained the howls and the footprints in the wet grass.

"Are you ready for school?" Aunt Marta asked. "Hannah will be here any minute."

"I'm almost ready," I replied. I gulped down a glass of orange juice. "When I was in the woods last night . . ." I started.

They both stared at me.

"I saw some animals that got ripped up. I mean, killed."

Uncle Colin nodded. "The woods are dangerous at night," he said softly.

"We really don't want you out there at night, Alex," Aunt Marta said. She pulled a piece of lint off the shoulder of my T-shirt. Then she tenderly brushed my hair back with her hand. "Promise us you won't go again."

"Promise," I murmured.

"And promise that you'll stay away from the Marlings," my uncle added.

Before I could reply, the doorbell rang. Hannah came into the kitchen, weighted down under a bulging backpack. "Ready?" she asked.

I nodded and shoved my chair back from the table. "Yeah. I guess I'm ready," I told her. "This is so weird. Going to someone else's school."

"You'll like my teacher, Mr. Shein," Hannah replied. "He's very interesting. And he's really nice."

I grabbed my backpack and my jacket. We said good-bye to my aunt and uncle and headed out the front door.

I glanced at the Marlings' house as we made our way to the street. The bedroom window at the side had been closed, I saw. The house was dark as always.

"Did you find your camera?" Hannah asked.

I nodded. "Yeah. But it wasn't easy." I told her about my scary adventures.

She *tsk-tsked*. "I warned you, Alex," she said. "You wouldn't catch *me* in the woods after dark."

A yellow school bus rumbled past. Some kids in the bus called out the window to Hannah. She waved back to them.

The morning sun still floated low in the sky. A silvery frost clung to the lawns. The air felt crisp and cold.

"One more block to school," Hannah said. "Are you nervous?"

I didn't answer. I was thinking about the Marlings. I told Hannah about the howls I'd heard inside their house. "Uncle Colin says they have two German shepherds. Really big and really mean," I told her.

"No, they don't," Hannah replied sharply.

I stopped walking. "Excuse me?" I cried.

"The Marlings don't have any dogs," she repeated. "I've lived here as long as they have, and I've never seen them."

"Then why did my uncle tell me that?" I demanded.

"So you won't be scared," Hannah replied.

"I — I don't understand," I stammered. "If the Marlings don't have dogs, what made those weird footprints outside their window?"

Hannah shook her head. Her olive-green eyes locked onto mine. "Alex, don't you get it?" she cried. "Haven't you figured it out yet?"

"Figured *what* out?" I asked.

"The Marlings are werewolves!" Hannah declared.

It's the season to be CREEPY!

Goosebumps®

BOOK AND STOCKING PACK

R.L. Stine

COMING IN SEPTEMBER

Make your holidays DE-FRIGHT-FUL with ten scary tales in the book MORE & MORE & MORE TALES TO GIVE YOU GOOSEBUMPS SPECIAL EDITION #6!

Available wherever you buy books.

GBSE397

Don't let any Goosebumps® books CREEP past you!

$3.99 EACH

Scare me, thrill me, mail me GOOSEBUMPS now!

Available wherever you buy books, or use this order form.
Scholastic Inc., P.O. Box 7502, Jefferson City, MO 65102

Please send me the books I have checked above. I am enclosing $_____ (please add $2.00 to cover shipping and handling). Send check or money order—no cash or C.O.D.s please.

Name_____Age_____

Address_____

City_____State/Zip_____

Please allow four to six weeks for delivery. Offer good in the U.S. only. Sorry, mail orders are not available to residents of Canada. Prices subject to change.

GIVE YOURSELF
Goosebumps®

...WITH 20 DIFFERENT
SCARY ENDINGS
IN EACH BOOK!

$3.99
EACH

Scare me, thrill me, mail me GOOSEBUMPS now!

Available wherever you buy books, or use this order form.
Scholastic Inc., P.O. Box 7502, Jefferson City, MO 65102

Please send me the books I have checked above. I am enclosing $_____ (please add $2.00 to cover shipping and handling). Send check or money order—no cash or C.O.D.s please.

Name_____Age_____

Address_____

City_____State/Zip_____

Please allow four to six weeks for delivery. Offer good in the U.S. only. Sorry, mail orders are not available to residents of Canada. Prices subject to change.

GYGB397